# The Sweeter Side of Deception

A Novella—Book One

## AVAGAYE CLARKE-HERON

InSPIRE PUBLICATIONS

minna PRESS

ISBN: 978-1-7324034-2-0 (paperback)
      978-1-7324034-3-7 (eBook)

Ordering Information
Quantity (Bulk) Sales: Special discounts are available on quantity (bulk) purchases by corporations, associations, and others. For details, contact: inspirepublications1@gmail.com

Executive Editor: Lena J. Rose
Designer: Mark Steven Weinberger

Published in the U.S.A.

# Dedication

I dedicate this book to my husband, Ricardo Heron, my main support system, whose impressive dedication to self-advancement, and believing in one's dreams inspired me to believe that I *could* author a book. And to my dear mother, without her decision to bring me into this world none of this would be possible.

# You Smiled, You Spoke, And I Believed

You smiled, you spoke, and I believed,
By every word and smile deceived.

Another man would hope no more;
Nor hope I what I hoped before:

But let not this last wish be vain;
Deceive, deceive me once again!

—Walter Savage Landor (1775-1864)

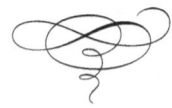

# Acknowledgement

I would like to express my appreciation to the many people who made the completion of this novella possible: to all those who provided support, offered comments, and assisted in the editing, proofreading and design.

I would also like to thank my publisher Lena J. Rose for her assistance in publishing this book. Above all, I want to thank my husband Ricardo and the rest of my family, who supported and encouraged me along the way.

To my good friend, and actor J. Zbek Nelson for his encouragement and faith in me. I started this novella some years ago, and the inevitable hurdles in life caused me to place it on the back burner for a while, until I sent it to my friend ZBEK. He was immediately intrigued by the story, even in its early stages, and encouraged me to get it completed. Thank you for sharing my passion and cheering me on along the way.

Last, but not least, I would like to thank all those friends, colleagues, and well-wishers who have been with me over the course of many years and whose names I did not mention.

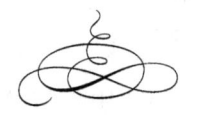

# Chapter I

Kayla woke to the scent of freshly brewed coffee; the smell perfumed the room with a hint a roasted hazelnut and fresh vanilla. The curtains were drawn, and sunbeams rolled in hitting her on the right cheek. She lazily rolled out of bed, sat up and then stumbled into the bathroom swaddled in the bed sheets. She ran the water for some minutes and gazed at herself in the mirror, "God I'm getting old," she mumbled to herself. Why do I keep doing this to myself, she thought. Why have I wasted so many years of my life on this man?

"I'll answer that," she said in a soft voice. "It's because you love him, and you still hope and believe that one day, he is going to realize that it is time to settle down. And when he does you will be right there, and he'll ask the question and you will say yes!" She turned on the faucet, letting the water run. "God I'm pathetic," she said. She cupped her hands and splashed cold water over her face. She let out a keening sound, like a wounded dog that's been kicked too many times, her words barely audible. "When will that day ever come?"

They had been dating on and off for about eight years, two of which were long-distance as Jay went away to New York for two years to help his brother, Ted, run the family business. Ted and his wife Celia were going through a divorce and Ted just wanted to get away. It was a rough patch for them, so Jay wanted to be there to help in any way he could and to give his support. At least that's what he told Kayla.

Jay wasn't from Vancouver, but Kayla was, so most of their time spent together was when Jay visited on business. When Jay told Kayla that he would be away in New York for two years, their relationship continued on a long-distance basis. Jay however, decided they could date other people during that time. She didn't date, but she would occasionally go home with some random guy she partied with on a Friday night.

Kayla remained devoted to Jay and she believed his actions seemed as if he was also devoted to her. Even when he was away, he would never forget her birthday and would send her thoughtful gifts. She would often get roses and jewelry on Valentine's Day, and on other occasions, stargazer lilies to remind her of how much he missed her. When he came back, to her it was like he had never left. From the moment they made love again, they just picked up where they left off. She kind of hoped things would have changed by now though, she was ready for something more than just being together. She wanted to know that it was more than being in love, more than having great sex, and oh was the sex great!

"Honey," Jay said, running up the stairs, "breakfast is ready." She quickly grabbed the towel, dried her face and ran her hands through her hair. He knocked on the door. "Are you in there?"

"Yeah, I will be out in a minute," she replied. He pushed the door open, and she turned around to face him.

"Good morning angel, how are we feeling this morning?" he asked as he moved closer to wrap his arms around her waist.

"I'm fine," she said with a smile. "The coffee woke me," He lifted her chin, so her lips could meet his.

"I made you breakfast," he whispered in between kisses, "your favorite... waffles, eggs and crispy bacons, just the way you like it."

"Hmm ... she whispered, "I can taste it already."

"Ok, then get dressed and meet me down stairs, I have a surprise for you. You will enjoy this weekend as long as I'm here." He gave her a big kiss on the forehead and headed to the kitchen. She went to the bedroom and dropped the sheets on the bed then slid into a little yellow dress and sandals.

He was at the table when she got there, making her plate. "Is this ok?" he asked" she smiled and nodded her head as to say yes, but her mind was still wondering when their relationship would get to the point where she wanted it to be? When would she get to have breakfast this way every morning? When would she have all her clothes up-stairs, her drapes in the living room and her pots in the kitchen cabinets?

"Are you OK baby?" He looked at her with concern, snapping her out of her runaway thoughts. He leaned over her right shoulder from behind and pecked her cheek. "Eat up now, remember I have a surprise for you after this, and I know you will like it, in fact you will love this entire weekend that I have planned for you..." She turned quickly and caught the mysterious smile tugging at his lips.

Could it be? She wondered, flushing with excitement.

After breakfast, Jay loaded the Jeep with foods, blankets, and other items that seemed very much like camping gear. "Are we going camping?" she asked in a curious tone, "I didn't bring any camping clothes, I... wasn't prepared to stay away from the house this weekend."

"Oh relax," he said. "I got it all figured out, besides I know you have jeans in the house, old tees and boots, and really that's all you need. Don't forget you also have me to keep you warm." He glanced at her from the back of the van with a dazzled stare in his eyes. "You'll be fine I promise, that's why it's a surprise."

Country music seeped from the speakers in the Jeep. The windows were down, and they were in love, just going with the mood of the wind. "How far till we get there?" Kayla asked.

"Just two more hours."

"Two more hours!" Kayla exclaimed, "We've been driving for almost three hours now. Where exactly are we going?"

"Can't tell you, remember it's a surprise," Jay replied. "Come on relax, I want to take you far away from the loft this weekend, I want us to spend our time somewhere else that's not so close to home. Besides, we stay in the house all the time when I am here, I just want to do something different. I want to give you a different experience; trust me, where we are going you will have loads of fun, and I promise you will never forgot this weekend. In fact, the rest of the surprise will make it a memorable one." He glanced at her and gave her a grin. She didn't feel that impatient anymore. If he's making this weekend extra special, one that she'd always remember, it could only mean one thing: He's going to propose. She turned and smiled at him.

"What?" He asked with a curious look on his face.

"Nothing," she said and turned away, trying hard to hide the smile that threatened to bloom across her face.

"Jay..."

"Yeah," he said, even more curious now.

"I love you..." Her voice hitched in her throat.

"I love you too baby, I love you too," he said dreamily and patted her hand.

It was evening when they pulled up at a cabin in the woods with a lake just beyond the trees. The sun made its gradual decline, leaving golden, incandescent shards of light shining through the trees.

"Wow! This is amazing," said Kayla, looking around her in wonder.

"I said you would like it."

"How is it that this is the first time I'm getting to know about this place?" asked Kayla, stepping out of the car.

"Was saving it for this very moment, to see that very look in your eyes, and it was worth it."

"I love you honey." Kayla began to tear up. "I never would have imagined that it would be like this, so perfect, so serene, so beautiful."

"Come on darling, grab that bag and let's go inside." Jay shut the trunk of the Jeep and headed for the door.

The cabin was made of pinewood that looked as if they were freshly varnished. The staircase, the tables and chairs, the cupboards, even the ceiling and the floors were all made from pinewood. "This is so beautiful," said Kayla as she glanced around. "Whose place is this?"

"It's mine... well ours," Jay replied. "I meant Ted and I, we bought it last year when he was going through his divorce. He didn't really want a home, he needed more of a place to get away. So, we bought it, and he was here while I was there taking care of the business."

"Oh, so is he moving here anytime soon?"

"No," Jay replied. "You know Ted will never leave that business and his kids to come live here. This is just for when he and maybe the kids want to visit to get away from the hustle and bustle of the big city, then here would be the ideal spot. Well enough about that, let's get you settled in so that I can take you to the lake, I want us to watch the sun go down together. Let's hurry."

"Oh, yeah, sure," Kayla stuttered as she followed him up the stairs.

They sat on the ledge of the wharf that evening. Jay wrapped her tight in his arms and they both watched the sun go down, the air filled with evening mist and fireflies. The water swayed back and forth as they swung their feet in it, they both said nothing they just watched and listened as nature said everything they both needed to hear.

"Jay thank you for everything, for this, for love… everything." She turned to face him, and he leaned in and kissed her.

"All of this means so much more to me when I'm with you," he said. "And believe me when I say that I wish it could always stay like this… always." The sun had finally slipped below the horizon, and the golden rays turned dusky. Darkness seeped slowly over the sky. With hands intertwined, they walked back to the cabin. Jay turned on the lights and lit the fire place. "It normally gets chilly at nights, so we got to get a head start with the heat."

"I want to take a bath; would you care to join me?" She tossed him a teasing smile over her shoulder.

"You're really asking me that? Would I ever refuse such a remarkable invitation?" They both chuckled as he grabbed her from behind and they both went up the stairs. Jay turned on the water heater and Kayla undressed to get into the shower. As she undressed, his eyes followed every curve on her body, from beginning to end. He bit his lips and walked over to her, and pulled her soft brown hair from her shoulders. He planted little kisses on the exposed shoulder. Her body inhaled whatever air it could get then she turned around to face him. He lifted her chin, kissing her fully on the mouth while his hands were busy cupping and kneading her breasts. A fire was igniting deep within her, he could tell. She moaned breathlessly as he lifted her and placed her next to the bathroom sink. Nudging her legs apart, he used his fingers to awaken her moisture. She grabbed him tighter, and her hips gyrated with every move his fingers made along her clit.

"Oh"... she sighed, as nectar flowed from her wetness. In a daze, she felt his strong arms lift her and took her to the shower. The flow of warm water flooded their heated bodies as he shoved her back against the shower wall. Her thighs were wrapped tightly around his waist as he buried his manhood inside her with the first masterful stroke. She gasped as she traced his bare back with her nails, moaning in great ecstasy and immense pleasure. Every stroke caused her voice to hit a higher octave. He flipped her around and with her back to his manhood he straddled her and plunged into her, over-and-over, without mercy. The intensity grew as she felt the throbbing inside her becoming faster and harder. She screamed, "pull my hair." He grabbed a tuft of her hair and pulled, and she moaned in wild abandon as the barrier broke that trapped their sweet juices of love.

Her body collapsed into his arms. Their steam evaporated slowly into the air, and she leaned her head to gaze into his hazel eyes. He gave a slack jawed smile, his light caramel skin glistened from the mixture of steam and sweat, his eyes hooded with the last vestiges of spent passion. "Must you always be this good?" she murmured dreamily.

"I aim to please and to satisfy," he responded. He slowly released her waist, allowing her slick body to glide down his hips and legs. When they stood toe-to-toe, he tipped her chin and looked down into her eyes. "So, are you pleased, and . . . are you satisfied?"

"In every sense of the word," she whispered, wiggling her hips for effect. Warm water washed away the remains of ecstasy that night. Sluggishly they crept to the huge bed. The sound of chirps and croaks was as relaxing as it could get, so they basked in the sleep music of nature as they retired into deep slumber.

# Chapter 2

Jay opened the blinds to greet the morning sun. Kayla shifted lazily in bed shielding her eyes from the inquisitive rays. "Wakey-wakey," Jay said in an energetic voice as he returned to their bed. Kneeling at the bedside, he asked, "did you sleep well?"

"Oh God, yeah," she replied yawning.

"So, what will we have for breakfast this morning?" he said playfully. "What shall Lady K have to eat?"

"Whatever Lord J, deems fit for the Lady," she replied, matching his playful mood.

"Not to worry, ma lady will be fed," he chuckled as he went down the stairs.

Her heart skipped as she remembered the steamy night they shared. He's got to propose she thought. Why else would this be so perfect? She rolled over in the bed with a soothing smile. I will never forget this night she thought, never.

After breakfast, Jay geared up the boat. "We are going fishing today, going to catch our dinner."

"Oh really?"

He nodded, a self-satisfied grin breaking over his face.

"We'll just see about that; besides I've never seen you fish before. For all I know this could be your first time." She threw her hands up toward the sky, "God, my dinner is in the hands of an amateur, I'm going to die of starvation!"

"I'm the captain of the sea," he retaliated playfully, "I'm a pro when it comes to fishing, you'll see, just wait and see."

He climbed onto the boat, and held Kayla's hand as she climbed on. "All aboard?" he shouted.

"Aye-aye Captain."

"Non-stop to fish land," he replied.

Kayla stared him down. "Really, that's all you've got… fish land." They both laughed as he started the engine and pulled away from the dock; the mist grew as they got farther away. After a while, Jay turned off the engine. "I think we are good here, this is where the fishes party," he said in an amused tone.

She laughed out loud.

"I love making you laugh, your smiles make me happy." He looked at her as if he was staring right into her soul, but with great distance in his eyes.

Jay placed the bait on each rod, and they both flung their rods into the water. "I bet you fifty dollars that I will get the first catch."

"Well aren't we confident," said Kayla with a surprised but excited look on her face. "Ok then, fifty dollars it is... and if I get the first catch, its double so you will owe me a hundred."

He shimmied his rod from side to side as if he had already caught a fish. "Game on... let's do this thing."

Some minutes passed when Kayla felt her rod pulling. "I think I've got one," she said with excitement.

"No, you don't," said Jay. "You're lying," he said playfully.

"Aren't we a sore loser," Kayla replied with much glee. She reeled in her rod to find a huge salmon dangling from the hook. "Well I've got my dinner, and I am a hundred dollars richer," she said gloatingly.

"You just got lucky... you newbies always get lucky... but luck's about to change."

"Don't worry," she said with mock sniffles. "You'll catch one soon, OK baby?" She laughed and turned her attention to reeling in the struggling fish.

By evening the catch was three to none. Kayla had caught two more salmon and Jay still didn't get lucky. The sun was dwindling so they packed up their fishing gear and headed back for home. The long day of fishing called for a hearty dinner, so Jay quickly got to cooking as soon as he got through the door. He cleaned and marinated the fish with spices and herbs and freshly squeezed lemon juice.

She watched as he moved around the kitchen, and she could only think how perfect this weekend had turned out to be. But tomorrow is Sunday, she thought, and soon it would be time to head back home. Work on Monday, is he waiting until the last minute? she pondered.

"Shall we?" Jay said, and she snapped out of her thoughts.

"Shall we what?"

"Shall we get our own selves cleaned up... I don't know about you, but I have fish all over me," he said.

"Of course, let's get cleaned up." They quickly left the kitchen and headed up the stairs for the bathroom. After a soothing bath, Jay went outside to light the grill and peel some potatoes. He sliced the marinated salmon and laid the slices on the grill.

"Grilled salmon and potato salad... how splendid," said Kayla, "I can taste it already."

Jay dropped the diced potatoes into boiling salt water and popped open a bottle of red wine.

"I like where this is going," said Kayla, as she took two wine glasses from the shelves. Jay poured wine into the glasses and they toasted to an exciting day and to a wonderful weekend.

Jay flipped the fish to the undone sides. He then drained the potatoes. Together they made a hearty potato salad, each adding their favorite ingredient to the salad, from sweet corn to sweet peppers, mayonnaise and crispy chunks of bacon. They were so into the moment, both giggling, hugging, kissing and playfully tossing the food that they didn't even notice the mess they were making in the kitchen. Dinner was finally served, and every dish looked and tasted fantastic. The salmon had soaked up every bit of the marinade and was oozing flavor. Every bite was an explosion of different flavors.

"Dinner is great," said Kayla, with her mouth full. "In fact, it's amazing." They both giggled, as they savored every last bit on their plates and every last drop of red wine from their glasses.

Dinner ended with two empty wine bottles, clean plates and satisfied tummies.

"Thanks for the fish," Jay said to Kayla, smiling at her.

"Thanks for a lovely dinner," Kayla said, kissing him on the lips, "I'll make you a deal," she said. "Since you prepared such a marvelous meal with those fish, you're off the hook, you no longer owe me a hundred dollars, you can keep it as a tip for the delicious meal." They both laughed. After tidying the kitchen, they went on the porch to the swing chair, Kayla sat in Jay's arms as they rocked back and forth, enjoying the masterpiece painted on the night sky. They reminisced on their lives, the times spent together and the events of the weekend. Laughter came to an end as drowsiness quickly overcame them. They retired to bed, wrapped in the warmth of each other's arms throughout the night.

At the crack of dawn, Kayla woke up. All night her dreams surrounded what would happen on Sunday. She must have gone through a hundred ways that Jay would propose to her and she wanted to be ready. She turned to kiss Jay on the cheek but surprisingly he was not in bed. Oh, she thought; the plans are already in motion. She skipped happily to the bathroom; she wanted to be flawless when he popped the question.

She got into the shower smiling, she was so anxious, where could he be so early if not to be up to something, some big plans. She hurriedly had her bath and applied make-up. Taking out the best dress she had in her bag, she laid it on the bed with matching accessories. After what seemed like an hour of preparation, she added the finishing touch; a splash of perfume. She headed down the stairs, her heart beating like a drum, and it was like everything was being played out in her head. She had already said yes before she reached the bottom of the staircase.

"Jay," she whispered, "Where are you?" She tiptoed into the kitchen, then onto the porch, and all the way out to the lake, but he was nowhere to be found. The Jeep was still parked in the driveway, so she knew he was there, but where? This must be a game, she thought as she walked back into the house. If she knew Jay well, he would want her to work for it. "I wonder if there are clues," she asked herself. "Come on K," she said in a motivating tone, "you can do this, just think." She grabbed the keys for the Jeep, not knowing where she was going, but driving was a start.

Perhaps he's somewhere up the road, maybe he has something planned in the town... she just had to see. She opened the door to the driver's seat and hopped in the Jeep. As she entered the key into the ignition she glimpsed a note on the passenger's seat. "Oh," she said as she smiled. "My first clue." Excitement and anxiety filled her heart as she unfolded the note... and began to read. Suddenly all that excitement quickly died down like a quick shower of rain on a blazing fire, and tears quickly followed as she read. On that sheet of paper were six years of answers that she had searched for during her entire relationship with Jay; and it read...

*Dear K,*

*I took you out to the lake this weekend to tell you about everything, but my heart wouldn't let me. Although I thought I could continue this I am now faced with an ultimatum. Kayla, believe me when I say that I truly love you and there is none like you, but the truth is there was one before you and she is my wife.*

*When I met you, my marriage was in shambles, I thought a divorce was the eventual outcome of it, but as the years passed by we eventually worked things out. I thought that what you and I had would have eventually worked itself out too. When my wife and I decided to let it work was the year I told you I was going to New York to take care of the family business with my brother. Actually, my brother is me, and his wife and kids and the divorce I told you about is actually all about me; 'my wife, our kids'. I had returned to sign the divorce documents* with our lawyers and to finalize the divorce settlement, but during all the chaos we realized that we still loved each other and that a divorce would not only hurt us more but also our children.

We rekindled the fire in our marriage for those two years I was away, and I only came back to let you know about everything. You were so kind and patient with me that I didn't want to hurt you. I just wanted to be honest once and for all. That night when I came back, I tried to tell you, but I also couldn't resist your charms and we made love. You reminded me how much you loved me, and I just couldn't find it in myself to tell you the truth.

I told my wife that I was just coming back for three months to sell the properties I had here, and tie up some loose ends in my business, and I did. Today is the end of that three months, so as you would have guessed I am now on my way back to my family. I sold the loft in town, I also sold the cabin, and I sold the Jeep along with it. I really thought that somewhere throughout these three months I had left here I could tell you the truth, face-to-face, but I couldn't, and that's why you are finding it out like this.

I will understand if you hate me, and if you never forgive me, but I hope you find it in your heart to forgive me. Trust me when I say I never meant for this to happen. I do hope you find someone to help you through this, and someone to love you the way you deserve to be loved. Know this, you will always be in my heart.

*The directory on the dining table is opened to the taxi service section. You can call anyone you wish, give them your location and they will come and get you. Again, I am truly sorry for all this.*

*Love, Jay.*

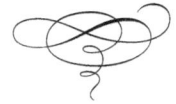

# Chapter 3

She crumpled the sheet of paper slowly in her hands, a still look on her face as the tears flowed even more. Dumbstruck, she got out of the Jeep and dragged her feet back to the cabin to pack her things. She dialed the first taxi service number her eyes latched on to. "I need a taxi" she said, not sounding like herself, "18 Lake View Terrace. Immediately." She stumbled outside, stood and turned to face the cabin; she gave it a deep stare and turned away. Her world slowly crumbled inside. She had no clear thoughts, it was as if everything was going bad inside her head, her body was shutting down and she could not do anything about it but to stand there helplessly and wait.

The taxi drove up about ten minutes later and she got in. "Cavern Town," she said… the driver nodded and drove off. Confused thoughts invaded her mind as she sat motionless in the back seat of the taxi. Her heart could no longer beat to the rhythm of happiness but to the rhythm of hate, lies and deceit. Her face had lost all its luster, and her heart froze into a thick block of ice. The happy Kayla everyone knew died with her heart that day.

After what seemed like an endless walk in a cave of darkness and complete silence, the driver asked, "Where in Cavern Town are you going?"

She stared at him for at least a minute before she could find the words to respond. "The condo on Oxford Street," she replied. The driver nodded and continued the drive. The car slowed down at the entrance of the condo and the driver got out of the car to assist Kayla with her bag.

"That will be eighty dollars," he said as he glanced at the meter. She quickly tried to dry her river of tears and pulled out a one-hundred-dollar bill. Keep the change she said in a muffled voice as she hurried away from the car.

She made her way through the doors of the condo as if the doors were not even there. With her head down, and her eyes blinded with tears she made her way up the stairs, completely ignoring the elevator and the fact that she lived all the way up on the 8th floor. The distance didn't matter she just didn't want to be around anyone, and the thought that the elevator may be filled with people irritated her. Before long she was on the 8th floor rustling through her purse for her apartment keys. In her mind, the words of that letter played over and over again making the simplest of things seem impossible and the shortest times seem like forever. The sound of the elevator coming to a stop on her floor made her rummage through her bags even faster. She angrily murmured under her breath for not finding her keys quickly enough. Finally, she found them in a small pocket within her purse. She turned the key in the lock and forced the door open. As soon as she closed the door, she collapsed on the floor to her knees with her back against the door and her hands holding her heart.

The sounds were faint but the tears flowing from her eyes soaked her cheeks and her neck, her body dropped face down on the floor as her fingers made fists that beat the floor repeatedly. Moans of loss and despair escaped from her muffled lungs. She cried and cried for hours, her heart pounding and aching more than she could ever imagine it could. From the time she got through the door she laid there in that one spot until it was night fall. The carpet area where she laid was as hot as open flames and soaked in tears.

She managed to lift herself up to the bedroom where she picked up the phone. The feeling of a swollen brain pulsating in her head was just one of the many pains she felt. She dialed the only person she knew could help her to come to terms with all that just happened in the last twelve hours.

The phone rang, and a distant voice answered, "Hello, Kayla is that you sweetie?"

"Yes, dad it's me," she replied with the crying tone in her voice, "it's me."

"Oh honey," he said, why... I mean what's wrong?"

"Are you home dad and are you alone?"

"I'm home and yes I'm alone… you know I am. Now tell me what is wrong with you and why is your voice muffled. Are you crying… what has happened to you Kayla?"

She couldn't help but feel guilty at the deep concern she heard in his voice. "I'm coming over dad," she sniffled like the five-year old she once was, who scuffed her knees after falling from her bike. Dad was there to make the pain go away. "I'll be there in the next thirty minutes daddy."

"It's too late for you to travel now, besides you left your car here so who will take you? What is wrong?"

"I'll be there shortly," she said. "I've always found my way before, I will find my way there now. She hung up the phone and grabbed her purse from the floor, beside it was her keys and her cell, and she picked them up and headed out the door. It was midnight, almost too late to catch a cab, but she was determined to be with her dad. There was no way she could bear the pain alone. Every possible thought of coping that ran through her head all ended with her lying dead somewhere from taking her own life. She just knew that getting a cab at midnight, in that part of the town, couldn't possibly be as difficult as all that she had experienced in the past few hours.

She stood there on the road side, shaking like a leaf, trying her best to block the chaotic flow of thoughts of the events that were swirling like a world wind in her head. She just stood still staring into the distance with the hope that a cab light would brighten the darkness and take her to refuge. After what seemed like about twenty minutes, a headlight beamed towards her, it was a cab indeed and she hopped into the car, "Pandora Street," she said.

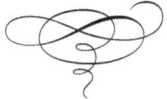

# Chapter 4

After a couple of minutes in the cab, Kayla directed the driver down the street to her dad's grey and white Cape Cod style house, perched at the end of a quiet street. She hopped out of the car and walked up the snow-covered path to his front door. Taking a deep breath, she knocked, anticipating her dad opening the peephole. Right on cue, the flap of the slider that covered the peephole opened.

"Oh, you made it," he said with a giant sigh of relief. "Come in... come in, you must be freezing." One look into her eyes, and he could tell something was terribly wrong. "Sweetheart, I have the kettle on to make you some tea. Just the right thing to warm you up." He kissed her cold cheek and helped with her coat. "It will settle your nerves too."

"No tea dad I just want to be here, I just want to...." She kept shaking her head from side to side while walking to the living room. As she entered, she briefly glanced around the room. It looked the same since she was a child.

By a big window, heavy, burgundy brocaded draperies hung straight from the ceiling to puddle on the weathered, wooden floor. Agitatedly, she paced back and forth, her fingers absently running across the back of the oversized, tufted leather chesterfield. She paused by the gilded fireplace mantel to pick-up a small, antique-framed photo and stared at herself. Her hands shook as she numbly placed it back on the mantle, beside her parents' wedding photo. Never would she be happily married like they were. Tears streamed down her face and she let out a strangled sob.

"Oh Kayla, what has he done?" Her dad said in a moaning voice. This will be the second time he will help to mend her broken heart. The first time was in high school, and she had vowed never to date another man. She didn't until she met Jay ten years later; fast forward past a nervous breakdown and an attempt to burn her high school lover's car. She was now faced with another situation that her dad noticed was much worse.

"He's gone Dad," she said in a shaky voice.

"What do you mean gone, did something happen while you guys were away? Is he hurt... Is he dead?" Turning slowly to face her dad, she pulled out a crumbled sheet of paper and handed it to him wordlessly.

"What is this?"

"Just read it dad," she said faintly. Her dad walked a few steps to the opposite end of the living room—an alcove dining room. He grabbed his reading glasses from the mahogany dining table that took up the entire dining area. Pulling out one of the eight, upholstered chairs, the wine color fading from disuse, he sat.

"Read it aloud," she said. Her dad looked at her and started to read. As he got further into the letter, he understood exactly what Kayla was going through. This was too much, he could no longer read aloud. Kayla was seated in the chesterfield with her hands clasped and her face down to her knees. "How could he do this to me? How? How could he do this to me? How?" Her voice sounding like a chant, breaking on the words and cracking like when she was recovering from laryngitis.

He dropped the paper on the table and slowly walked over to her. "You'll get past this, you are stronger than you think."

"Am I dad, "will I truly get past this?" Pain was slowly giving way to anger. "He will pay for this dad. He - will - pay!"

Her dad couldn't find the words to console her. He knew that Kayla was deeply in love with Jay, and made it known to him that he was the one she would marry and grow old with. He silently blamed himself for not seeing the type of man Jay truly was. He wondered how he could have missed the signs as he hugged his daughter. As she nestled her head on his shoulder, he also wondered how would she come back from this?

He glanced at the grandfather clock in the corner; it was almost 2:00 am and Kayla had fallen asleep in his arms. Slowly he stood and laid her down on the chesterfield. He went to the bedroom and chose a blanket to cover her. Turning off the lights, he sank into his favorite, plaid recliner, rocked backwards, and extended the foot rest with a loud creak. As he listened to her ragged breathing, he could only imagine the depth of pain she must be feeling. His heart sank as he replayed the words of the letter in his head. What he couldn't understand was how someone could be that heartless? How could Jay claim to have loved her and hurt her like this? Oh boy, what would he have done to that bastard if he had seen him before he left town. He grounded on his back teeth in frustration, his jaw rigid. If he could feel like this, he could only imagine the seed of vengeance growing in his daughter's heart.

Kayla woke with a start to the sound of her father calling her name. "Kayla... Kayla... it's almost 6:00 am., Love." He noticed her face was momentarily free from the previous night's anguish. "I know this must be a silly question, but I'll ask anyway, what are your plans for to-day? Did you make arrangement with work to be off? If not, you need to do so or go home so you can get ready before 8:00 am."

"Oh work," she said, rubbing the sleep from her eyes. "No, I didn't make arrangement to be off today, I don't think I can be around anyone for a while dad..."

Before she could finish the sentence, her dad said, "I would rather you be around people Kayla, this is what you need, distraction to get your mind off this. Tell me, would you really want to sit around here all day and replay what happened and relive the hurt. Or would you rather be at your desk getting some work done, that will at least place your thoughts on something else; even if it's just for a short while?"

She looked up at her dad annoyed, but she knew he was right. "Ok, I'll go home and get ready."

"Great. So, are you coming back here tonight? Should I make dinner?"

"No dad, I think I'll stay home tonight, besides knowing my job, I probably have a desk full of portfolios that I'll need to take home to finish. I'll call you when I get off, and when I get home." She gave her dad a peck on the cheek and walked to the bathroom.

When she was ready and leaving, her dad stopped her at the door, "Kayla," he said, "I love you and I also know you, you are a strong individual, what you need is a fresh start, find a way to start thinking of this situation as a distant past and everything else will work out."

She hugged him. "Thank you so much for being there for me always, especially when I need you most."

Kayla arrived at the office around ten minutes after 8:00 am. Avoiding direct eye contact with anyone, she walked to her office. With help from her coffee cup, she held her head down taking sips as she made her way through the chatter and groups of co-workers filling each other in of their various rendezvous over the weekend.

Just as she had thought, a pile of files greeted her as she opened her office door. Great... she thought, I swear Matthew thinks I'm the only Client Advisor in this office.

Kayla was great at her job, she worked with one of the largest wealth management companies in her region and was known in the office as the go-to guru. When it came to managing the portfolios of some of the company's wealthiest clients, there was just something about her that made her know how to maximize client engagement. She understood her client's needs on both the client's level and the company's level. Somehow, she found a balance where she could make everyone happy by responding to the exact banking needs and providing wealth advice that her client(s) require. Her level of expertise in her job meant that with every new, affluent and high-end client the company gained, their portfolio would end up on Kayla's desk. New clients also tended to ask for her by name, which meant her reputation was known by many.

Placing her cup of coffee on her desk, she opened her window blinds. Her office had a beautiful view, from the 5th floor and her office window overlooked the city park. In the distance, she could catch a glimpse of Rice Lake in Metro Vancouver where people would often relax and take in the beauty of the area. As soon as she entered the office each morning, she would take a deep breath and enjoy the view. This ritual would often kick start her day, but not today. She opened the blinds and the first thing that she saw were couples on the park bench, she felt like someone stabbed her heart. A knock sounded at her door. "Come in," she said as she rustled the blinds shut.

Matthew, Kayla's boss, walked in with a big grin on his face. As the Lead Relationship Manager, he was the primary contact for the company. He was in charge of handing over the clients' portfolios to the Private Client Advisor he thought could best handle the clients need; this often meant he would hand over the clients to Kayla.

"Kayla, I have great news."

"Let me guess, you met with some top-notch clients over the weekend who agreed to let DMC manage their wealth." She rocked back on her heels, looked him dead-in-the-eye with a self-satisfied smirk on her lips. Folding her arms across her chest, she said, "and now you want me to take them on... don't get me wrong, Matthew, I love what I do. But don't you think the other advisors would love to have some of these high caliber clients in their portfolios too?"

"You're funny," Matthew replied, completely dismissing her remarks. "Anyway, that's not why I am here. Come on sit down we need to talk opportunities." Kayla sat and leaned back in her high-backed, executive chair, her hands together with her forefingers almost pointing to the ceiling. He sat in one of the chairs in front of her desk and made a 360-degree swivel then faced her. "So, I met with Bernard over the weekend, you know... the CEO of DMC."

"Yeah, what did you guys talk about?"

"I'm getting to that. So, DMC is expanding its California office, which means they are targeting a larger client base, which also means they need the best to target and get those wealthy Californian clients." He raised his hands like a stop sign. "Now, before you say anything, you know California has some of the richest clients in that region, and this would be an opportunity for you to transfer into a promotion." He waited to let that settle in her brain before continuing. "Bernard agrees that based on your track record and reputation among our local clients, you would make a great Client Relations Manager for the California office. We are talking about six figure salary, paid relocation and accommodation for a year, the ideal office, and you have complete control of the training and hiring of client advisors." Phew!" He blew out a breath. "There, I spilled it all out—one shot. Are you impressed?"

His eyes beamed with excitement.

Kayla took a second before she responded. "Well, two things: (1) Why are you so excited about me leaving and moving to California? And (2) What about my life here, what about my clients?"

Matthew looked at her as if she was asking the wrong questions. "Well if you should know, I'm excited because you are my best advisor and I want nothing but the best for you. Besides, you'll still be a consultant for this location so in a sense I'll still have you," he said jokingly, spreading his palms apart. "Kayla, you know I've always looked out for you, no one else has put in the time and dedication you have in the past years you have worked here, other than me" he pointed out in a reasonable tone, "Look, you deserve this, and I will not sit around and let this opportunity of a lifetime pass you by. So?"

"You expect me to give you an answer now? Matthew this is all so much, so sudden, you must let me think about this; besides I have a life here you know. I just made an offer on the house we talked about, and my money is in escrow, plus my dad... what about my dad? I can't just up and move a million miles away, I'm all he's got."

"Snap out of it Kayla! All I'm hearing are excuses to pass up on the opportunity of a lifetime, something I know you have been dreaming about. Don't forget I've known you like forever and I know this is what you need to push your career to the level you have been working so hard for. So, stop making excuses and give me an answer, and don't be too long because they need someone in that office within the next month, which means you must make that decision now so that relocation plans can begin. Look, I know its short notice, but a great opportunity doesn't always come with an advance notice. So, get yourself together and have an answer for me by the end of the week." He abruptly rose from his chair.

Kayla said nothing as Matthew opened the door, tossed her a reproachful look and walked out of her office. She took a deep breath and buried her head in her hands. She knew within herself that he was right. She had been working towards an opportunity like this and it was really the promotion of a lifetime.

She imitated Matthew by swiveling her chair, thoughts careening through her brain. Was she ready to move to a new country and start all over? It's not because she wasn't capable of handling that promotion, but because she wasn't ready to deal with what it would take to get over the hurt to be able to function as everyone would expect her to. She mustered up what little drive she had left in her and started sieving through the mountains of new client portfolios on her desk. Her mind replayed everything Matthew had said, and what her dad had said about needing a fresh start. As she went through the events of the past days, over and over, she made a decision. Now she needed her brain to convince her heart that it was the right decision. She ended the day with only two client folders left untouched on her desk, she made a sigh of relief and switched off her computer. It was a quarter to seven, and she realized she had spent the entire day at her desk with not even a bite to eat. She quickly grabbed her bag and headed out the door.

As she walked through the office she could see that almost everyone was gone except for Matthew. She walked up to his door and knocked hesitantly. "Come in Kayla," he answered.

She stepped into his office. "I'm off for the evening, I emailed you a detailed report of the new clients you wanted me to report on, except for two whose portfolios require a bit more research. So, I will get those done in the morning and follow-up with the report."

"I know. I'm going through the report now and I couldn't agree more on the proposed investment options. Well done. So, have you placed any thoughts on what we discussed today?"

"I have, and I will have an answer for you by morning. I just need to think things over tonight."

"Ok. I'll see you then, take care and have a great night." As she walked out of his office, he raised his voice, "And get some sleep!"

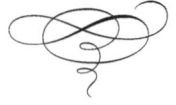

# Chapter 5

Matthew was already in her office, waiting for her when she walked in the next morning. "Somehow, I'm not surprised you're here," Kayla said with a slight grin on her face.

"Great, so that means you know why I'm here. So, what's your decision?"

"At least let me sit down please." Besides you said I'd have until the end of the week to give you an answer, today is Tuesday."

"Oh no, no, no. All that changed when you told me yesterday that you'd have an answer for me today. I believe your exact words were, "I'll have an answer for you by morning." Hence the reason I'm here, because I'll be dammed if I'm going to give you room to change your mind."

"Change my mind? You are talking as if I'd already said yes."

"Oh, don't patronize me. I know you have already decided so I need to hear you say it so that I can update Bernard."

"Fine," Kayla said. "I've decided not to take the offer."

"What!"

She laughed. "Calm down, I'm just kidding."

He held his heart as if he almost had a heart attack. "You'd better be kidding."

"Yes. I've decided to uproot my life and move to California."

"Ok, great. So, you know things are going to get crazy around here for the next couple of weeks before you leave, right? You'll need to fully hand over, brief and update Shannon, who will take over from you. You'll also need to meet with a couple of our high-profile clients, the ones who only want to see you when they come here—just to let them know that you'll still be consulting with us from the California office. That way they'll have peace of mind." Matthew was going on and on about a hoard of things that Kayla needed to do and all she could see was his mouth moving. She couldn't hear a thing he said. She was too zoned out just thinking of how her life would drastically change over the next few weeks. When her wandering mind finally returned to the conversation, Matthew was scheduling a department meeting for their first briefing.

"You got that?"

"Got what?"

He rolled his eyes. "The date for the departmental meeting," he said slowly, as if speaking to a nit wit. "We need to do that first so that we can inform everyone about your promotion and get them up-to-speed with the events that will transpire over the next couple of weeks. As you prepare to leave, trust me you're going to need all the help you can get."

"Sure." Kayla responded, still a bit confused. "When did you say again. Friday at 11:00am?"

"Put it on your calendar Kayla." Matthew shook his head from side-to-side as he left her office.

As her computer came on, she quickly added the departmental meeting to her calendar. She couldn't help but notice all the other meetings and appointments that were scheduled in her calendar for the week. She scratched her head as she viewed them, knowing the barrage of items she would also need to do to smoothly hand over to Shannon. She made a big sigh and delved right in.

The days flew by, and soon it was Friday. She found herself walking out of the departmental meeting with a sense of accomplishment. She had a clear path to tackle the upcoming weeks leading to her transfer. What was most gratifying to her was how everyone was rooting for her and seemed genuinely happy that she was promoted. "You've got this." she whispered to herself as she sat at her desk. The weeks indeed came fast, and went as fast as they came, from client meetings to staff briefings, to take-over trainings, she was swamped. On the last week before her transfer, she sat in Matthew's office as he went over the itinerary with her and what to expect when she landed in California the following weekend.

"So," Matthew said smiling at Kayla, "when you land at Los Angeles International Airport next Saturday, your assistant Lisa Bryant will be waiting for you at the airport. I have sent a picture of her to your phone, just so you can have an idea of what she looks like. She will also have a pick-up card with your name on it, so it will be easy. You will be staying at the Hyatt Regency at Los Angeles International Airport (LAX) for the first week, just until your corporate apartment is ready. Lisa will go over the details of that with you when you get there. You will be using a rental also, for the first week until you are all set in the new apartment then a company car will be provided. All expenses for the trip and stay will be covered as you know, and if there are additional expenses not account-ed for in the first week of allowances you can record and amend accordingly.

Lisa will help you work that out with the company's CFO in the event you need to."

Kayla nodded. All she could think of in that moment was that this is life altering. Her stomach fluttered.

"So, I notice you are not saying anything," Matthew said gazing at Kayla to make eye contact.

"I'm just lost in thought. But I got all you said, and

I am well-versed with the itinerary. After all, this is our third time going over it."

"So, I was thinking"... Matthew interjected. "Since we are all clear here, the hand over was successful, why not take the rest of the week off, it will help you to get your things together and at least spend some additional time with your dad before you go."

"That would be great. God knows all I need now is time."

"Then it's settled. "I will see you at the sendoff party on Friday, so go home, rest, think of what you need. This is not a vacation, remember this move will be your new home for as long as you remain Client Relations Manager for the California office. So, you have permission to go overboard with the packing," he chuckled. Kayla gave him a small smile. He continued, "besides, they are paying for it so go knock yourself out." He hugged her. "See you Friday," and she made her way out of his office.

The send-off party was very emotional for Kayla. She may have been locked in her little bubble of a confusing relationship so long that she didn't even notice the love and respect, so many others had for her. She knew by the end of the evening that she was leaving behind some great friends, colleagues, and well-wishers. Though she didn't want to admit it to herself, her heart felt a bit warm, she was happy.

Kayla spent the few days of the remaining time she had left with her dad, who fully supported the move and convinced her it would all work out for the best. Though she also tried to convince herself that the move would help her to heal, she still had doubts. She thought of the possibility that she'd be lonely in California having no family there and no friends. Would that be the ideal environment to get over a broken heart? Would moving to California magically make her forget all that had happened to her? These were just some of the questions she battled with, questions that she just didn't have the answers for, and it scared her. She found comfort in telling herself that she didn't have much to lose and a lot to gain.

The Friday before her flight, she sat in her apartment staring out the window as the rain poured. She couldn't help but feel that nature was mocking her, or somehow imitating her emotions. She walked over to the bed where she had been packing a small travel bag. Among the clothing on the bed was the little yellow dress she wore the day Jay took her to the cabin. She held the dress and just stood there staring at it. "Six damn years of my life!" She screamed angrily as she tossed the dress across the room, she had purposely omitted the other two years he was away. "Six years, and all I got was a thoughtless explanation scratched on a piece of paper of why my heart was not good enough, a failed attempt at justifying why I deserved to be hurt by love." She swallowed hard. "Was I wrong for loving him?" she asked herself, "Is it wrong for someone to give their all to someone they love and trust? She knew within herself that she was venturing back into the dark cold cave of her vengeful heart, but at that moment she didn't care. She had been putting on a smile for everyone for the past month, but deep inside her heart was aching. Her heart was ice cold, and though she could hide the pain in front of everyone else she couldn't lie to herself.

Thoughts ran through her head of all the questions she wanted to ask Jay, of the things she would do to him if she ever saw him again and they made her angry. So much so that her body shook, and chills ran down her spine, and the scenarios of the murder she would commit played out in her mind. Her phone rang, she quickly dried the tears from her eyes and cleared her throat when she saw that it was her dad calling. She didn't want him to know she was still crying. "Hey dad," she said as she answered the phone, trying to quickly sniffle away the sound of her tears.

"I'm just checking on you Kayla. Just want to make sure you are ready for tomorrow."

"Yeah dad," she said hastily, "I'm here packing."

"Packing?" he asked, "I thought you did that days ago."

"I did. I packed the big stuff and most of my clothing and those were shipped ahead of my trip. But I'm just packing a small travel back pack with a few clothes and toiletries and other necessities just in case my bags aren't ready when I get there." She chatted with her dad for a while. They both had a lot of emotions and it all poured out in goodbyes and well wishes.

"I love you dad."

"You just take care of yourself baby girl, and don't forget this is a new chapter, write it well."

Her dad hung-up and she held the phone close to her heart. She pulled the covers over her legs and turned out the lights. I'll try dad... I'll try to write it well she whispered to herself as she fell asleep.

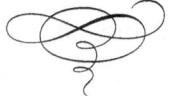

# Chapter 6

It was not until Kayla arrived at LAX international airport late Saturday evening that it really sank in that she was starting all over in a brand-new place. She took a deep breath as she walked towards the slender brunette who stood in the middle of the airport with her name on a sign board. She was very pretty and well-dressed as if she had just walked off the pages of a fashion magazine. Kayla managed to form her mouth into a smile as she got closer to her. "You are Lisa I presume." Kayla said, reaching out for a hand shake.

"Yes. And you are Kayla Riviera?"

Kayla nodded in agreement as they shook hands.

"It's my pleasure to meet you Miss Riviera. I'm looking forward to working with you." Lisa turned and signaled the driver that was waiting by the exit and he came and took the few bags Kayla had with her.

On the short drive to the hotel, Lisa began to run Kayla through her schedule for the upcoming week. It was a lot, but Kayla had anticipated it would be, so somehow, she wasn't worried. She was however happy when Lisa told her that the personal items that she had shipped prior to her move had arrived and were waiting for her at the hotel. The more Lisa spoke, the more Kayla was impressed. Lisa seemed to have everything together and it was not just her competence, it was her hair, her clothes, her diction, how organized she was. Kayla liked that about Lisa and she thought to herself that she had a great assistant which made her smile a bit.

She settled into her room after Lisa left. She flipped through the color-coded organizer that Lisa gave her out-lining all her meetings for Monday. After a shower, she called her dad to let him know she had settled in. He was very happy to hear that she had landed and settled in. After they chatted for a bit she hung up, and opened the screened door that led out to a balcony. The night lights were beautiful, and in a sense calming. She stood there for a while just breathing in the night air and clearing her mind. Though she had not yet seen the entirety of this new place, she could imagine starting over here and it felt good.

After a few seconds of standing on the balcony she heard a knock on her door. The concierge had come to check if she had needed anything and invited her down for dinner. She was indeed hungry, so she told the concierge she'd be down. It didn't help that she was the only one sitting at a table in the restaurant. For a moment it sent her back into a dark lonely space in her head. She hurriedly ate dinner, as she felt everyone was staring at her and maybe thought how pathetic she looked dining at a five-star restaurant alone.

She didn't hesitate to crawl into bed when she got back to her room. Burying her face into her pillow, she was mad at herself for walking into a position where her heart could reminisce the hurt. It seemed the harder she had worked not to feel, the harder the universe tried to overthrow her efforts. She grabbed her phone and looked for her favorite playlist, she upped the volume and shoved the earphones in her ears. It didn't matter that the volume was deafening, because it helped her to not think of anything else, and that's exactly what she wanted.

On Sunday she ordered in breakfast and lunch from room service. She did spend most of the day by the pool reviewing her strategy brief for one of Monday's numerous meetings. Spending her time drowning in office work at a resort would have once seemed like a waste of quality time to her, but now it was a way to escape. Later that evening concierge rang her room to let her know that a table was reserved for her at another of their fine dining restaurant. A live band would be playing. Her first instinct was to cancel, but as the concierge spoke further of the events for the evening, she remembered what her father had said. Moving to California was her new chapter and that she should write it well. "Thank you," she said to the concierge. "I'll be there."

After what seemed like an endless search through her luggage for something formal to wear, she managed to get to the restaurant a few minutes before 7:00. It was a little different than she had imagined. Being a fine dining restaurant, she had expected everyone to be seated, stiff-necked at their tables listening to jazz or classic rock from the live band. To her surprise, the music was upbeat, yet tasteful. People were dancing and mingling, and she didn't feel as if everyone was staring at her. Frankly, it looked like everyone was just having fun and minding their own business.

The evening seemed to pass by effortlessly. On the walk back to her room, she hummed a catchy instrumental the band had played. She couldn't believe she had danced with a total stranger and was practically happy all evening. Maybe she could forget, maybe she could start writing a new chapter, maybe. Back in her room she selected an outfit to wear for work the next day. It was sophisticated, yet stylish and the perfect outfit to play the part of the 'new manager.' She laid out two outfits over the arms of her bedroom bench, one, a sleek well-tailored all black pant suit, and the other a knee length red dress that was fitted and tapered to her body with a sophisticated detailing at the neck. It had just the right fit that when she wore it you could tell she was a powerful woman who knew how to dress, it showed just enough of her curves but not too much to be unprofessional. As she stood there staring at the two outfits she knew the pantsuit would demand respect, but so would the red dress, and it would also show that she was approachable. The email notification from her phone broke her chain of thought. Lisa sent her a reminder that she would be at the hotel at 7:00 am with the driver to pick her up. The email also had a brief reminder of her schedule for the day, and a list of documentation and reports she would need to have ready. She smiled at the thought of how anal Lisa was, but she loved it. 'Noted,' she typed in her reply to Lisa. The remainder of her schedule seemed to have helped her decision in her choice of outfit. She chose the red dress because, other than being sophisticated she could also get away with being in it all day comfortably, as opposed to the pantsuit.

The following morning, she didn't wait in her room for Lisa to alert her. She was dressed and waiting for her at an area she knew they would see her as they drove in. They were right on time and she was prepared to listen to Lisa's updates for the entire ride to the office. Her first meeting was an introductory meeting where she would meet all her new staff. Lisa walked her through a list of who would be there, their positions and recent accomplishments in the company and even their field just in case she wanted to highlight anyone. Kayla took a deep breath as she walked into the conference room. This was a big deal for her, the first impression everyone would now and later have of her all depended on how well she presented herself at this meeting.

Lisa smiled at her as she walked from the podium, "you did well," she whispered. Kayla smiled at her. "Thanks." The rest of the day was mapped out with meetings. Kayla found herself running from strategy meetings, to board meetings, to client introductions. Lisa was right there guiding her through.

That day had formed the foundation for her role at the California office. She sat in her new office exhausted from the day's events. With a sigh of relief, she felt good that she made a great first impression. Through everything that had happened in her life, she never thought she could stand in front of so many people so soon and exude confidence. Lisa knocked on her door before walking in, and she was quickly snapped out of thought. "Well that's it for today. The driver will be waiting for you, it was a great first day, now go home and get some rest as the real work starts from here on."

Kayla smiled at Lisa. "Thank you. You have been of tremendous help, and you were a great part of making this day successful. So, I'll see you tomorrow?"

"Yes boss," I'll be here when you get in."

Days turned into weeks and weeks into months. Kayla kept busy, consulting with the Vancouver office, and getting the California office structured to the point where it was operating efficiently. But when the smoke cleared, and everything was organized enough where she didn't have to work long hours and weekends, she realized that there was a lot missing in her life. To keep her personal life separate from her work life, she never fraternized with her colleagues. She refused all invitations to office outings and other personal invites from her colleagues to various excursions. This wasn't her home, at least she wasn't that familiar with the place yet, so she didn't know many places to go and unwind. Some nights she felt trapped in her apartment which made her think of how different her life would have been if Jay had not deceived her. The dark place she so desperately tried to keep her mind from venturing was where her lonely nights often took her.

One early Friday evening as she was getting ready to close from work, Lisa came to her office to give her some documents she had requested. When Lisa was about to leave, Kayla stopped her at the door. "This may sound silly," she said, "but would you happen to know of a place I could go to unwind around here? Somewhere refined where I can get a few cocktails without wondering if there are people from the office watching me?"

Lisa smiled at her. "Of course, I will send you the links to a few places I know that's classy and exclusive. You can review them and decide on one that best suits your needs."

"I would really like that." When Lisa left, Kayla sat in the office until she knew everyone was gone, then she headed back to the lonely place she called home.

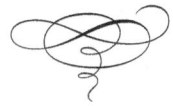

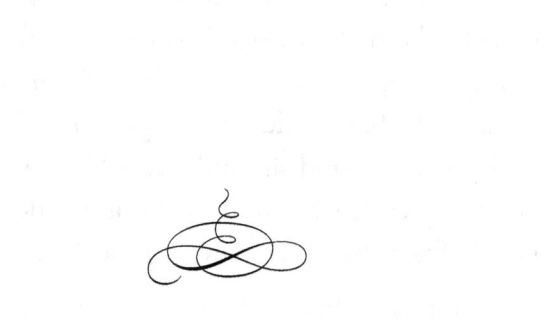

# Chapter 7

It took Kayla a while to muster up the courage to go out by herself. After months of passing the place she chose from Lisa's list, one evening she decided it was now or never. She ruminated and debated with herself.

"What do I have to lose?"

"It's not like anyone here knows who I am, or my pitiful story for that matter."

"How will I start writing my new chapter if I don't turn the page?"

She took a deep breath and walked across to the entrance of the lounge. She had registered for months and was now just attempting to go in. The lounge, called *WhisPer*, was an upscale hang-out spot. To gain admission, she had to complete their application online which required one to be earning a substantial income, fit a profile, and lived in selected parts of California. After applying, a background check would be done and if qualified, one would have to pay an annual membership fee. This meant that only a selective clientele, both in wealth and societal class could gain access.

She fumbled in her purse for the access card that they had mailed her some months ago. She swiped the card at the door and her name appeared on a digital monitor built into the door. The words, *access granted* ran across the screen and the door opened for her. When she entered, it was like something she only saw in the movies. She could see why the vetting process required a background check. The layout of the lounge was unimaginable. The décor included crystal countertops, marble floors, million-dollar lighting and chandeliers, seats made from the finest leather and the ambiance was like a dream. Her eyes caught a large screen that was displaying some features of the lounge. Her mouth dropped open when she saw some of the things being featured. She was even more intrigued that they offered private spa sessions, unlimited cocktail hours, and a full fine-dining restaurant with renowned personal chefs. She quickly saw that this wasn't her typical lounge, it wasn't just bar and a club, it was like an exclusive resort. As she stepped further into the lounge, a hostess approached. "Welcome to *WhisPer*, Miss Riviera, we've been expecting your visit for some months now." Kayla stuttered for the words to respond as she was caught off-guard.

"I'm just getting around to it," she quickly responded. She was a little surprised that they could identify her, then she remembered the background check.

"I'm Keturah, I'll be your personal hostess throughout your membership with us. Based on the preferences you selected during the application process, we have prepared a personalized booth for you. A mixologist is assigned to make your requested cocktails, one of our in-house masseuse will be at your disposal and a chauffeur is also assigned should you need one. In your booth, you will find a tablet, you will use that to communicate with me throughout the evening as I will not be in your personal space. Should you need me, just use the hostess app to send me a message. You may also use it to communicate with the rest of the staff to request the services you will need for the evening. You will receive a series of notifications on your tablet as the evening progresses to let you know what events will be taking place, where and when. Follow me please." Kayla walked behind Keturah, a bit blown away by all she was hearing, she knew it was an upscale lounge, but she was amazed by the level of exclusivity and features.

Keturah led Kayla to her private booth, and the booth was decked out to mimic the ambiance of a nature trail. From the music to the paintings, the color scheme and the fresh pine scent, it was like she was sitting on the boarded deck at the lake after a trail walk. She could hear birds chirping in the background, soft music and the swish of water. It was so calming it was like her head instantly cleared the moment she walked in. She realized that Keturah was now quiet and only stood there smiling as she took it all in. "It's beautiful," Kayla said trying to break Keturah's silence. Keturah did not reply but acknowledged her compliment with a smile. Keturah proceeded to type something on a tablet she had, and as soon as she had finished typing, a notification popped up on the tablet she had earlier told Kayla about. Keturah gestured to Kayla to pick up the tablet, and the notification was a message on the screen which indicated to Kayla that beyond the doors of the client's private booth, the hostess, along with the rest of staff does not speak. All communication beyond that point should be initiated by the client via the tablet.

Kayla responded to the message to let Keturah know she understood while another indicated that Keturah would be leaving but would be available anytime. Kayla smiled as she took off her jacket, and cozied up in one of her lounge chairs. Intrigued by all the cocktail options she had, she didn't hesitate to start her order. In less than a minute of requesting her first cocktail, the mixologist was there with her drink. Within an hour, she had drunk over twenty cocktails and she just kept ordering.

For the first time since her heartbreak, she had gone through an entire hour without feeling the ache of the open wound in her heart. The memories of his horrific deception ran deep. The truth is, she was wearing a mask that told everyone around her that she was fine, that she was the woman who had everything under control, but deep down she was dying inside. Deep down she was wrecked from the ordeal, deep down Jay's deception had torn her to pieces. She was but a fraction of the woman she used to be, there was never a day that she didn't secretly have a mental breakdown in her head just reliving that dreadful day. But, for the first time in months, she had gone an entire hour without remembering, probably it was because she had numbed her brain with alcohol. Maybe it was because there wasn't a thing in sight to play on her emotions which often led her to remember. She didn't know what it was, and maybe drowning herself in cocktails wasn't the best way to get over it, but it was a start.

Needless to say, *WhisPer* became Kayla's second home, or maybe, even her first. For the five months that she had now been in California, she spent most of her evenings at the *WhisPer*. It was more time than she spent at her corporate apartment, so much so that other high-profile clients began to notice her. Though she was being noticed, she avoided making any friends. She preferred to stay in her booth at each visit, and only mingled when she went on the dance floor or when she was dining at the restaurant. One Monday evening after a rough day at work, she scheduled a spa treatment at *WhisPer*. As she laid on her back with a mud mask on her face and infused cucumber slices over her eyes, she heard a voice that she knew wasn't her attendant. "You must be having a rough day to be at the spa on a Monday," the voice said. "I'm usually the only one in the spa on a Monday. It's good to know that I'm not the only one who have crappy Mondays, crappy Monday's is an understatement for that matter. I think I have a crappy day every day of the week." The person continued chatting to the point that Kayla began to get slightly annoyed. She laid there thinking that maybe if she kept quiet the person would stop talking.

"I'm Elizabeth by the way," the woman continued, and with that said, Kayla felt the cucumber slices being removed from her eyes.

Standing over her was a feisty looking redhead. She was very beautiful which was Kayla's first thought, and she had gorgeous skin. She seemed like she was in her mid-thirties, and almost reminded her of Julia Roberts from *Pretty Woman*. With her eyes gleaming and hands outstretched for a hand shake, she said, "my friends call me Liz."

Kayla noticed that it was Liz who had removed the cucumber slices from her eyes. Kayla sat up and acknowledged her by responding, "I'm Kayla." They shook hands and Kayla laid back down on the spa bed.

"You are not much of a talker, are you?" Liz asked. "I notice that you come to *WhisPer* a lot, I don't mean to pry but for someone… well the women I know and from my own experience who come here a lot, only do so because we are trying to escape the pressures and pains of the real world. We try to escape a crappy marriage, some a crappy boss, heartbreaks, crappy relationships, and the list goes on. So, what are you trying to escape, what's your story?"

"I don't have a story. I'm just trying to relax."

"Well my story is a crappy marriage," Liz replied in a tone that almost let Kayla know that she wasn't going to shut up anytime soon.

Liz went on and on about how she had filed for divorce twice from her cheating husband and both times had let him talk her back into staying. "Always saying he would change, but he never really changed" she said angrily. "He pretends to be God sent and sincere every time we get back together but when he knows that I've totally accepted him back, he starts cheating again. It's like it's a game for him and I'm just tired of it all, tired of being used, tired of being treated less than I really am." Kayla was laying there almost trying to zone Liz out, but when Liz started crying it struck a nerve in her. She suddenly thought, here is a woman who doesn't know me, a total stranger pouring out her heart to me to the point of crying and I'm here trying to ignore her. She started to think about her recent heartbreak and how she had poured out herself to her dad. She could relate to what Liz was going through, being used and taken for a ride.

Kayla could see the pain emanating from Liz's eyes. Quickly she rushed to sit next to Liz and pulled her into her arms. She realized Liz just needed to vent so she held her like she had needed to be held when Jay broke her heart. Kayla said nothing, allowing Liz to empty herself, just being the shoulder she needed to cry on. As she sat there consoling Liz, it was unknown to Kayla, this evening would be the genesis of her own healing, the beginning of a different kind of love.

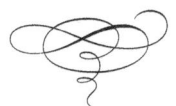

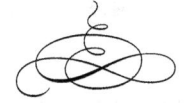

# Chapter 8

After that Monday evening at the spa, Kayla and Liz started sharing each other's company even more at *WhisPer.* They would alternately hangout at each other's private booth and on weekends they would attend a few of *WhisPer's* high-profile parties. Kayla didn't mind Liz's company, but she didn't think they were that close yet to open up to her. Liz, however, had no problem spilling the beans on her marriage, and the pains her husband James was putting her through. Maybe Kayla felt bad that the man she was so madly in love with, who eventually broke her heart had turned out to be married man. She didn't know what Liz's impression of her would be. Would she hate Kayla for not knowing that he was married? She knew she hated herself for not seeing the signs. He was practically living in two countries, interchangeably, and she just blindly took his word for it that he was travelling for business.

One evening as they sat together in Kayla's booth, Liz was upset that James didn't even care about what their constant fighting was doing to their children. Kayla wasn't quite sure what to say, but she did wonder, if James was such a bad husband, a narcissist, a neurotic cheater and abuser as Liz often claimed. Why then did she take him back more than once? Kayla tried to wrap her mind around it then she finally asked. "Why did you take him back the second time? I mean you said you filed for divorce twice, I can maybe understand forgiving him the first time, but why the second time? Seems to me that he's taking you for granted because he knows you'll always forgive him." Liz paused and looked at Kayla, and she went quiet for a moment and placed the cocktail she was drinking on the table. Looking at Liz's saddened face, Kayla immediately thought she had said something wrong. "I'm sorry if I overstepped Liz, I didn't mean to. ..."

Liz quickly interjected. "Oh no, you didn't overstep, it's more like you hit the nail on the head. He is taking me for granted because he knows that I'm afraid of being alone. The thought of starting over scares the life out of me and he knows this. Plus, in the earlier stages of our marriage, he had made somewhat of a personal sacrifice for my father's legacy to continue. I might have told him then that I owed him my life, which he now hangs over my head like some sort of a control switch. I will tell you how it all went down.

We met in law school about ten years ago, he was studying to be a Civil Litigation Lawyer and I was studying Estate Planning to someday work in my dad's firm. My dad started and operated one of the best Estate Planning firms in California with some of the best legal personalities on his payroll. Along with that, he was a real estate guru, managing billion-dollar properties, both within and outside of the United States. When I was in my final year of law school, my mom died, and it took a toll on me, James was there for me through it all. My dad delved deeper into his work and started travelling more in and out of town for work. Being an only child, it was like I was all alone. James took on the role of my dad, my mentor, my support system, he really stuck by me almost jeopardizing his own studies just, so I'd stay sane enough to complete mine. When we both graduated, James proposed, and of course, I'd expect it because we were inseparable.

"But, of course," Kayla murmured in encouragement.

Liz closed her eyes and sank back in the plush leather booth. She took a deep breath then her eyes popped open and she continued her story. "James wanted to start his own firm, so he had quickly returned to school to complete his Masters of Laws. A year into our marriage, I became pregnant with my daughter Charlotte, so I put my plans of getting my Masters of Laws behind me for a while. That same year my dad suddenly died from a major heart attack, and I need not say I was devastated. Here I was, a new wife, a new mom and an orphan. My family legacy, my dad's companies were all left for me to run. I couldn't do it, I couldn't pull myself together to be the mom my daughter needed, much less to talk of running my dad's companies. I was also very aware that in the jurisdictions that my dad operated his firms and real estate companies, for me to be eligible to be an executive lawyer in his companies I would have had to have my Masters of Laws degree. I was certainly in no position to go back to school at that time. James knew what I was going through and he switched his major from Civil Litigation to Estate Planning and Real Estate. He did this for me, just so he could step in to keep my dad's companies from crumbling, and most importantly, to keep the management of the firms within our family. I knew how much he wanted to be a Civil Lawyer, to start his own firm, and I knew that giving up that dream to run my dad's companies was a huge sacrifice."

Kayla massaged the beads of water gathering on the outside of her cocktail glass. Glancing up at Liz she said, "how gallant of him – doing all this for you, huh?"

"Oh yes. From then on, I had a new level of love and respect for him and I never hesitated to let him know how appreciative I was and how indebted I was to him. Our marriage was going fine until he was required to go on a restructuring project for my dad's firm in Vancouver. For the next six years of our marriage he was in and out of our lives spending most of his time in Vancouver. At first it didn't bother me because I knew it came with the territory, I had watched my dad live this way for years, but what got to me is that he started to change.

"How so?"

"After a while, Kayla, whenever he would come back from Vancouver it was like we didn't matter anymore, he didn't touch me, he didn't want to spend time with his daughter. To make matters worse, I had reached out to one of our partners who was a part of the restructuring team and he told me that the restructuring process had only taken them a little under eleven months spread across two years. That meant that for the other four years that my husband was spending months at a time in Vancouver in the name of work was a sham."

Kayla shifted uneasily in her seat. Wow. Their lives were kind of parallel in that way. Lies. Damn lies.

Liz looked off into the distance, her eyes vacant as she dredged the rest of her story from the depths of her soul. It was as if she'd never given voice to her pain and it was all splattering out now in one big vomit. A thin film of sweat shone on her face with the effort, but she squared her shoulders and continued in a drone-like voice. "When I confronted him he denied everything, and didn't hesitate to let me know how ungrateful I was for all he had sacrificed for my family. Can you believe..." she smothered the caricature of a laugh. "He said, how lucky I was to have him for a husband. I knew I had lost him then because the James I knew before would have never thrown that in my face. He wasn't there for me or our daughter the way he used to anymore, and I decided to file for a divorce." She studied her perfect white-tipped manicure, buffing each nail, then gave a wry smile that never reached her eyes. "I served him with the divorce papers, and what do you think he did?"

"He refused to sign?" Kayla asked with a shrug.

"He came back, and he begged, Kayla, he literally begged me! He promised that he would try to be better, to be there for us. He confessed that he had made a mistake and had an affair in Vancouver and that he had put a stop to it and he would be back home for good. Believe me, I was hurt, but then, I was foolish enough to take some of the responsibility for his infidelity."

"No, you didn't. How were you at fault?"

"Oh Kayla, by believing him when he said that if it wasn't for me and my family he would not have been in that situation in the first place. Well, we rekindled our marriage and I have to say that things were better --for the next two years. I mean, he was home, he was there for us and he was the James I had met and fell in love with. During those two years that he had put Vancouver behind him, we had our son David. I then decided if I was to keep my marriage the way it was, I needed to make an executive decision to close the Vancouver firm. I wanted to sell the properties my dad had there, and also relinquish the property management responsibilities of the real estate holdings. In my mind, this was a fair decision to save my marriage from a repetition of what had happened before." She chuckled without mirth. "But to James, I was being vindictive, and he fought my decision for months. I couldn't understand why he couldn't see where I was coming from. Why was he so bent on keeping the option open to travel back to Vancouver? This led me to do some digging and it was just as I had feared, he was still in the relationship he told me he had ended."

Kayla covered her mouth with her hand, resting her elbow on the table for support. Speechless.

"Girl, I found text messages, credit card statements of money he was spending on her in Vancouver, I even found bills where he was sending jewelry and gifts for this woman. At this point Kayla, I had had enough, and I gave him an ultimatum, it was either he cut all ties in Vancouver by going with my decision to close the companies there, or we get a divorce. To prove to him that I was serious, I filed for the divorce. Knowing a thing or two about family law, I included a clause my dad had used for years. Basically, without ties to the family, whether by blood or through marriage, James could not hold an executive position within the firms or any of the family businesses. If he did choose the divorce, he would also have no claim to my family legacy, ultimately he would have been left with nothing."

"You got him there, didn't you?

"By the balls!" She flung back her head with a throaty laugh. For a moment she seemed like she had it all solved. Her voice took on an exhilarating lilt. "He swore on his life that the woman was the one still holding on, and that the gifts were incentives for her to let go. He even said that the only reason for not wanting to close the businesses in Vancouver was because having them would be beneficial to our children's future. He swore he only wanted to make us happy. To prove to me that he was sincere, within three months he went to Vancouver and liquidated our properties. He closed the firm and was back with us." She paused, the weight of it all pressing down her shoulders to create a slight droop.

"Well?" Kayla looked at her expectantly. "It didn't last did it?"

"Ha!" She sprang back to life, as if coming out of a trance. "Now fast forward almost a year later he is cheating again, I know it's not the woman in Vancouver because I have done my checks, but there is someone else I just know it."

"How do you know for sure that there is someone else?" Kayla asked.

"Because he's acting the way he does when he cheats. He neglects his family, he gets verbally abusive, and he spends more time away from home. The only reason I haven't filed for a divorce yet is because we both signed an agreement. You see, after I had called off the second divorce, I didn't trust him anymore. I got so paranoid... so much so... that every move he made I accused him of cheating. After a sit down with our family lawyer, we decided in a signed agreement that the only way I can file for a divorce, ever again, is if I get physical proof of my husband's infidelity. In the event I try to file for a divorce without physical evidence, James gets half of everything my family owns."

"Oh no." Kayla slapped her hand to the sides of her head as if trying to knock sense into Liz's head.

Liz shrugged. "I am basically stuck in this hell hole of a marriage, James is using this agreement to his advantage. He's being extra careful to not leave trails, yet rubbing it in my face. I believe it's some sort of a revenge because I made him break-off his affair in Vancouver."

After telling Kayla her story Liz broke down crying. "I just want to be happy" she sniffled. "I just want to wake up to someone who loves me the way I deserve to be loved." Kayla understanding exactly what she meant tried to console her,

Kayla hugged her fiercely. "James does not deserve your tears, and for what it's worth, I believe anyone one dumb enough to take your love for granted is not worth your love at all." Liz's head was snuggled to her bosom as she sobbed. After some minutes of crying, Liz disentangled from the embrace. She dried her eyes, held Kayla's hands and looked her in the eyes. "Thank you for being here for me," she said, "I really appreciate it."

Kayla reached out to hug her and in a split second their lips interlocked. Liz had kissed Kayla, and funny enough Kayla was kissing her back. For the few seconds that the kiss lasted, Kayla's mind went through a whirlwind of thoughts.

What is really happening?

It was so wrong, yet felt so right.

What would happen next?

Was this kiss the start of something new. or the end of their friendship?

# Chapter 9

After that night's kiss, things got a little awkward between Kayla and Liz for a few days.

Kayla's year in her corporate apartment was coming to an end and she needed help getting her own apartment. She had asked Liz to help her out, and Liz was more than happy to do so. Unwittingly, Liz was filling the emptiness inside her.

After a month of searching, viewing and narrowing down prospects, Kayla finally decided on an apartment. Liz having connections in the real estate industry helped her to get the best deal when she closed on the property. Liz was now fully practicing law in her dad's company, as she had completed her Masters of Laws over the years her husband was working in Vancouver. She had wanted Kayla to enlist her firm for her future needs in estate planning and property management, but Kayla told her she would think about it.

After purchasing her condo, Liz had volunteered to help her move. They had gotten close, so much, that they practically did everything together. Kayla knew almost everything there was to know about Liz, or so she thought, but she never told Liz the details of what really happened to her in Vancouver at the hands of a man. Maybe she was still embarrassed, or maybe it was her way of not reliving the past. Kayla learned that Liz's children: Charlotte and David mostly stayed with Cathy, their grandma, who was James' mom. Cathy had taken the children so that Liz and James could work out their differences. Kayla knew intimate details about Liz, what made her happy, what made her sad, things she liked and things she hated. The most Liz knew about Kayla was that she had moved from Vancouver to California for a promotion. Kayla only had her dad as her mom died when she was younger. Kayla was also deeply hurt by a man back in Vancouver that she had loved. Kayla didn't go into details of her life with Liz, but she told her just enough so that they could both understand each other.

The night Kayla was moving into the apartment it was raining hard. It had rained all week long. They had arranged the furniture in the apartment earlier that day, more to soothe Kayla's taste. They still had to gather Kayla's bags and other personal belongings from the corporate apartment. It was about nightfall when they dashed in with the last of Kayla's things. They were soaking wet, so Kayla offered Liz some dry clothes. After a while they settled on the couch, sipping their hot chocolate and giggling over nothing. They had been dabbling in awkward foreplay some months after the kiss, but had never managed to go all the way. As the rain poured outside, they suddenly went silent and just sat there staring at each other. Liz leaned in and began playing with Kayla's hair. Kayla sat her mug down on the coffee table and they slowly caressed each other. Liz took control, gently kissing Kayla from the neck down. She slipped her hands into Kayla's silk nightgown and groped her left breast using her hand to gently massage Kayla's nipple. Kayla swallowed hard, her eyes closed at each kiss and touch.

Liz travelled down the length of Kayla's body with her tongue. When she got to Kayla's navel, she was rewarded with a deep inhale. Slight moans escaped Kayla's lips as Liz's hands found its way between her legs. Liz laid her down on the couch and slipped off her lace underwear, she buried her head between Kayla's thighs, tasting the sweet juices. With great gusto, Liz' tongue licked and circled Kayla's pink clitoris, turning it cherry red. As she played with Kayla's clitoris, she slipped her fingers deep inside her vagina, her fingers thrusting and moving to the rhythm of Kayla's hips. Kayla grabbed Liz's hair. Her moans heightened as Liz's fingers thrust harder and faster while her tongue followed in sequence encircling her clitoris. Kayla's legs shook while her grinding hips came to an abrupt halt as she reached her peak and climaxed. She pulled Liz's face up to hers, and in a final tongue lock, her body collapsed into Liz's hands. This night was the start of many others like it, and the two fell deeply in love.

James' constant unfaithfulness only pushed Liz closer to Kayla, and the hopes of them working out their differences was erased from Liz's mind. She did everything in her power to get physical proof his infidelity. At times, she felt guilty knowing that she was somehow being unfaithful too, having fallen in love with Kayla. She found comfort in telling herself it was under different circumstances as he pushed her away; besides, she knew his heart was no longer with her at least that was how she felt.

One night, Liz started an argument with James so that he would leave the house. She was desperate to get proof, and so she had Kayla tail him the moment he left the house. Kayla sat in her car a block away from Liz's house waiting for the car Liz had described to her. They had gone over the plan more than once before that night. For Liz to get her divorce without risking half of her father's legacy, they had to catch James in the act.

Kayla was supposed to tail him and get evidence of whomever he was going to be with that night. Kayla followed James' car to a house about an hour away from his home. She called Liz. "He's getting out of the car. I've got to go, I'll call you back."

It was a bit dark, so Kayla knew she had to get closer if she was to get a clear video of James and of anyone he was going to be with. The house had large windows and glass sliding doors that made it almost easy to see inside. She waited in the car until James went inside the house then she sneaked up close to a window where she would be able to get a better view. James was indeed with a woman, but she needed to see his face, and his back was turned to her, so she could not get a good view. She could however see the woman clearly, and she was a bit surprised that he was cheating on his wife with her. She was beautiful, yes, but she was not as beautiful as Liz. Though she couldn't yet see James' face, she thought it would still be wise to get a picture with the woman's face, at least for Liz. She snapped a quick picture of the woman before she ducked back down under the window.

When she slowly stood up again, the couple had already moved to another room. In that room, the light was on and Kayla near crawled on her belly to get a good view of them. As easy as it was to see them; they could also see her too. She had to be careful, so she slipped behind a rose bush that was at the right side of the yard facing the glass door. She was sickened by how James was all over this woman. How easy men found it to deceive the women they claim to love? She laid there, praying for a clear shot of James' face so that she didn't have to see any more of this treachery. The way he pushed the woman up against the glass door reminded her of the way Jay used to handle her body when they made love.

Demanding.

Masterful.

Rough.

A shiver ran down her spine, the longer she thought

about it, and she felt embarrassed that she was getting aroused thinking about him. She shook off the feeling and lifted her head to continue videotaping the couple. She froze. A jolt blasted throughout her body, like she was being hit by a bus. She sank to her knees, dry-heaving short, panting breaths while the phone dropped from her hand.

Her mouth opened and closed, soundlessly, like a fish. A thousand bees swarmed inside her head buzzing questions:

"How? How could this be?"

It all didn't make sense. It didn't add up. All lies. Lies. Lies.

It seemed like forever, but the buzzing finally stilled in her head. An eerie quiet followed as the truth settled into her bones.

Liz's dirty bastard husband, James... *was her Jay.*

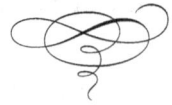

# Chapter 10

She fumbled around in the grass for her phone. With trembling hands, she scrambled to take the last footage of them in the act. Satisfied, she caught clear views of their faces. Her mouth twisted in an evil, triumphant grimace of a smile, then she slithered like a snake away from the rose bush and ran to her car. Still reeling from shock, she had trouble getting the keys into the ignition, her hands were shaking so badly. When she finally turned on the ignition, she hurriedly sped away from the scene.

She tried to make sense of it all. In the letter Jay left her, he had implied that his wife's name was Celia. From what Liz told her he was a Lawyer, yet he told her he was an IT Consultant. He had been lying to her about everything from the beginning, not just withholding the fact that he was married, he even lied about his name. It all made sense now, referencing Liz's story, putting the pieces together excluding all the lies. She finally understood, she was the woman Liz spoke about in Vancouver that had an affair with her husband for over six years.

She couldn't help but think that even though she was a victim of James' deceit, she was also somehow the cause of Liz's pain. The hurt, the anger, and the bitterness she had tried so hard to put away all came rushing back to her mind. Rage burned inside as she thought of how he had used them both and without a sense of remorse. Now he was doing the same thing to another woman, who probably also thinks the world of him and who had not the slightest clue that he has a family. Her phone rang. It was Liz. She cleared her throat and answered.

"Did you get anything?" Liz asked with much enthusiasm, Kayla paused for a while. "Yes, it was exactly as you have thought, I'm heading back to you now, I'll see you soon." When she hung up the phone she couldn't help but wonder if Liz knew that she was the woman in Vancouver. She remembered Liz telling her that she had done some digging and found credit card statements, and text messages verifying the affair. She wasn't sure, but she couldn't help but wonder if Liz knew.

When she pulled up in the driveway of Liz's home, Liz was standing there, waiting for her. She took a deep breath before getting out of the car. Walking towards Liz she tried to conceal the look of pain and slight guilt that was written over her face. Liz walked to the door and stood anxiously, switching her weight from one leg to the other as Kayla approached. "I'm so nervous to see the footage you have, but, yet, so happy at the thought that I'm not paranoid for believing he was still cheating. Have a seat, I'm just going to get us some coffee."

As Kayla sat there waiting for Liz to come back, she pulled up the last video file she took that showed clear footage of James and the woman being intimate. She couldn't understand why she couldn't shake that feeling that Liz might know of her and Jay/James relationship. Liz handed her the coffee and she could clearly see that Kayla wasn't fine. "Are you alright?" Liz asked.

"I'm... fine," Kayla stuttered a bit. "It's nothing really, I just believe I let what I saw get to me a bit more than it should."

"Oh Kayla, its fine," Liz responded trying to calm her down. "Don't let it get to you, I mean I know you would find him cheating. I've made peace with this, so don't feel bad for me, if that's what this is about. Just think about it, Kayla, with this proof, I can get the divorce I need. James cheating ass won't be able to lay a claim on any part of my father's legacy, and we get to be together."

Kayla forced a smile and handed her the phone. Liz hit play on the video and her reaction was not what Kayla was expecting, she was smiling instead of looking hurt. "That's not the reaction I was expecting. Liz, I mean why are you smiling, how does seeing this not hurt you?"

"I'm smiling because I know who she is."

From the tone of Liz' voice, Kayla now understood that she was deeply hurt by what she was seeing.

"I know who she is," Liz repeated with a feral gleam in her eyes. She pursed her lips and stabbed a finger at the image. "She is our family lawyer, the attorney that handled the first two divorce filings I made. She is also the one who suggested that we sign the agreement I told you about? That's the agreement where I had to have physical proof of James's infidelity if I were to ever try to divorce him again—that would be the only grounds where he wouldn't be entitled to my family's assets."

Kayla's eyes nearly popped out their sockets. "That dirty bastard," she whispered. "There is no end to his deception."

"None! I can't believe the nerve of that bastard!" Liz screamed, "screwing our family lawyer all this while. I bet this was going on a longtime. I bet this is the reason she suggested this twisted divorce agreement. I bet she wanted James to get half of everything my father labored so hard for... that bitch."

Kayla was at a loss for words. She had initially felt that this woman may have been deceived by James like she was, but now learned that this was not the case. This woman knew that James was married, and knew everything about his family. She was their family lawyer for God's sake! How could the woman not know? Kayla was so confused she just sat there looking at Liz with concern while inside she was burning with rage. Jay/James was now in her reach and she just wanted him to hurt the way he made her hurt. "So, what now?"

Liz pushed the phone away from her on the cocktail table as if it was tainted. Several beautifully illustrated art books laid carelessly on the table for effect. A single white orchid towered over the arrangement to give a refined air to the luxurious monochromatic living room. She sat back in the plush couch and worked her bottom lip with her teeth. "Well for starters, I want the divorce now more than ever, but I'll have to get another divorce attorney, since this bitch of a family lawyer is the one screwing my husband. I'm not worried though, I know plenty of divorce lawyers, this divorce will be finalized within three months, tops. Then, I'm going to sue that bitch for violation of trust, alienation of affection, and criminal conversation. She'll be lucky if she can still practice law in California when I'm through with her."

Kayla listened to how Liz was planning to destroy her family lawyer. She swallowed at the thought of what Liz would do to her if she knew she was the Vancouver mistress. At the same time, she knew it was not her fault and that she was deceived by Jay/James. If she was to continue an honest relationship with Liz, she had to tell her; but the timing was all wrong. Liz was dealing with so much, she didn't want to open another can of worms from the past. She quickly stood up and checked her watch, "Liz, I'm sorry for everything, but I know that you are on top of this and you'll be OK. I've got to go now, as you know, I have work tomorrow. You know that I'm here for you, so if there is anything else I can do just let me know. As we had discussed, now that you are going to go through with the divorce you'll be around your family more for the transition, so I know we won't be seeing each other as often as we were until the divorce is final." She looked deep into her eyes and whispered, "but I know we'll make it work."

Liz stood up to hug her and thanked her again for helping her to get proof. "I can't wait for this to be over," she said. "I can't wait for us to be free and open with our relationship.

Trust me when I say, I'll get started on this divorce right away and I'll update you every step of the way. Thank you for understanding and thank you for everything." For a while they hugged each other passionately as if they didn't want to be separated. They said their goodbyes, kissed and Kayla left.

The next day, Liz sat in her living room dressed for work, waiting for James to walk through the door. She watched as his car pulled up in the driveway, the entire time she sat there twiddling her thumbs just waiting to descend on him. She had barely slept that night, just going through all the things she wanted to say to him. Now that she knew for a fact that he was still cheating and who he was cheating with, she couldn't wait to confront him. When James walked in and saw her sitting on the coach, the look on his face told her he wasn't expecting her to be there.

"Good morning," he said sheepishly, avoiding eye contact and making his way towards the staircase.

"Not so fast," she said.

"Oh, here we go again," he rolled his eyes and stopped in his tracks.

"Oh, don't worry, my dear husband, this won't take

long at all. I just want you to know that I'm filing for a divorce, you'll hear from my lawyer by the end of the day."

He looked at her almost annoyed. "Elizabeth we've been over this, a million times, I'm not stopping you from filing for a divorce, you know the terms of filing for a divorce. I know I have not been cheating on you, so if you are paranoid enough, and is ready to mess up our family and go through the hassle of splitting assets then by all means be my guest."

"I was counting on you to deny that you have been cheating" she said with a smirk. "You are right, I am paranoid and that's why it's going to give me great pleasure to see your face when you finally see that you're about to lose everything." She sashayed towards the cocktail table and tossed him a saccharine smile over her shoulder. "And, oh, James darling, you may want to check your phone, and..." She paused and turned to face him, a fake pout on her lips. "As I said, you will be hearing from my lawyer by the end of the day. And, oh, before I forget, you may want to give your mistress, our dear family lawyer, a heads up." She walked deliberately now, as if dismissing him, but not before a parting shot. "Do, let her know she'll be hearing from my lawyer too," she said in an even *sweeter* tone than before.

James was dumfounded. Without another word, she picked up her car keys from the coffee table and left. He stood there for a moment when she left, he searched his pockets for his phone, but it wasn't there. He went outside to the car and found it. He saw the notification on his phone from his Liz. He got back inside the house where he reluctantly played the video that Liz had sent. His heart dropped when he saw the footage, and he knew right there that this was the end of the road. He couldn't think straight, he just kept pacing back and forth in the living room with his hands on his head. He knew exactly what this meant, and there was no way he could fix it. Knowing what he had put Elizabeth through for the last couple of months, he knew there was nothing he could possibly do or say that would let her stay this time. He collapsed at the foot of the staircase, with his head pounding and heart racing. He dialed Celia's number; their family lawyer; his mistress, and the only thing he could say to her was, "she knows."

# Chapter 11

In the next few months, Kayla and Liz mostly communicated over the phone. They tried their best to see each other over the weekends, but it was not like before. They did manage to stay intimate, with each other, on a few occasions when they'd meet up. But with the divorce in its final stage, it was just a matter of time until they were back together.

Though it wasn't fun for Kayla, not being able to see Liz as freely as she wanted, she was still a bit relieved that she had some time away to think things through. Now that she knew the truth, that Liz was Jay's/James wife, she had a decision to make. She loved Liz and she didn't want to be the one to hide a big secret like this from someone she loved, she knew too well what it felt like to be deceived.

She knew if she kept this from Liz it could turn out terribly wrong. Eventually she would have to come face-to-face with James, since Liz decided to share custody of the kids with him. But she also thought that if she told Liz about it now she could face the risk of losing her and the chance to confront James. Liz had discussed with Kayla that she would have to introduce her to James as a formality in the custody agreement being that she would be in a relationship with her and ultimately the kids. She didn't want to lose the opportunity to see the look on James face when Liz introduced her as her lover, the one who would be replacing him. The more she thought about it, the more she knew that she had to hold off on telling Liz the truth until after the 'introduction' with James.

Some weeks later, Kayla was getting ready to meet Liz at her house, the divorce was final, and Liz was moving out. Though James got nothing from the business and property side of the divorce, Liz had decided to leave him with the house as it had too many bad memories for her. When Kayla got to the house she rang Liz to let her know she was outside. The door was open, and she entered. She didn't know whether James would be there, or not, because Liz didn't say, and she didn't ask. But, she knew it was a possibility and either way she was prepared. As she walked through the front door, she immediately realized that he was there, she could hear them arguing upstairs. She could somewhat hear what they were saying, and she knew James was not happy. Her heart pounded against her ribcage as she walked gingerly to the staircase. She could hear raised voices and she listened while they argued.

It sounded as if the couple were in the bedroom and, Liz was packing the last of her things. James was trying to convince her that she was making a huge mistake. "You know this is ridiculous," he said in a furious tone.

"No James, what's ridiculous is me taking your shit for all these years, all in the name of not wanting to be alone, all in the name of being grateful. The truth is, James, I loved you through it all, and maybe you once really loved me but that was a long time ago. Your love for me died the moment you started that affair in Vancouver. We both know that. I hated you for letting someone destroy what we had, and I hated that woman for coming in between us. But I still didn't let go, because, yes, I was scared to be alone, scared to lose the life I had built with you for all those years. Even when I knew you no longer loved me I held on and I tried to love you. But you didn't love me back, you proved to me that you loved her, and you spent the rest of our marriage punishing me for breaking up your silly affair. But you know what James? I'm not scared anymore, because I found someone who loves me, the way I deserve to be loved, and I'd rather take that chance on love, than suffer in alienation with you." She gave a throaty chuckle. "Why am I even here talking to you? The divorce is final, we have both signed and sealed it, now I'm taking the next step to be happy. And, you know what James? you should be happy, happy that I didn't take full custody of the kids like I could, and happy that I wasn't bitter enough to leave you without a home. You are still a lawyer, and I can't take that away from you, so instead of you standing here whining about me being ridiculous, why don't you be grateful that at least now you get to go chase your dreams like you really wanted. Now you get to sleep with everything in skirts, without me being in your way, or better yet, go back to Vancouver and go find the woman you truly love."

There was a long silence and Kayla knew that James must be just standing there with his mouth agape or he was ruminating on his wife's words. Finally, he began speaking again. "Do you really believe that another man will genuinely love you the way I have, with all the flaws I loved you with, are you that naïve?"

Another brief pause ensued before Liz said, "you know what James? That's where you are wrong, I will never trust another man because you are all the same. For your information, I found a woman that does love me, the way I deserve to be loved, with all my "flaws" as you put it. And don't for one moment think that I owe you any explanation as to who I date, because you lost that right the day you started cheating on me. The only reason you will be meeting her today is because of the custody agreement. We both get to know who each other will be having around our kids. She's downstairs waiting for us, so I suggest you come meet her and get this over with, I need to get on with my life.

Kayla heard them getting ready to come down the stairs. She backed away from the staircase as she heard them coming. She stood a short distance from the foot of the stairs where she knew he would see her the moment he came down. Their eyes connected the instant he came into view. With the shock of seeing her, he tripped causing Liz to stagger. Liz turned and looked at him almost annoyed. She then turned and looked at Kayla and smiled. "This is the last of my things," she said to Kayla. "The rest of my bags are in the garage, and I'll need your help getting them packed in the car." Liz turned around to look at James who was trying to hide the shock on his face. In Kayla's mind it was priceless and exactly what she had expected it to be. "James this is Kayla, the woman who makes me happy. The woman who loves me flaws and all. Kayla this is my ex-husband, James." Liz then turned and looked at James and back at Kayla with a gleaming look on her face that neither of them understood.

Kayla nodded at James with a smile on her face. James stood there dumbfounded and still in shock, both said nothing, and the silence was as thick as the black of night. "Let's go Kayla," Liz said, breaking the silence. "Let's leave James alone to enjoy his new-found freedom."

Kayla knew it was now or never to say what she wanted to James and she pulled Liz aside and whispered in her ear. "I will meet you by the car. I need a moment with James."

"Why?" Liz asked.

"Just trust me. Everything will make sense in a while, just trust me."

When Liz left and closed the door, he blurted out, "Kayla!" with an expression of confusion and disbelief. Before he could get another word in Kayla stopped him, she walked up to him and their faces were almost touching.

With a grin plastered on her face, she whispered, "I bet you thought you'd never see me again." James opened his mouth to say something, and she silenced him with her finger closing his mouth. "You don't get to speak," she said, "you said all you had to say in that letter you left me back in Vancouver." Her heart was racing, but her rage was gone, there was so much she wanted to say, but it suddenly didn't matter to her anymore.

"It's funny," she said, "when you left me at that cabin, I was so filled with rage I spent most of my days thinking of all the bad things I wanted to do to you, for all the pain and hurt you had put me through, and trust me they were some really bad things. But, like fate would have it, I moved here to California to start over, and I met Liz, and then not having the slightest clue that she was your wife, we fell in love. And I forgot all about you and what you did to me, until that night when Liz asked me to tail you and I caught you cheating. You could imagine my surprise that sure enough, Liz's James was the same Jay who left me in Vancouver after wasting almost eight years of my life. Karma is a bitch isn't it? Having proven Karma to be true, I can totally forget about what you did to me. But you know the irony of it all? You will never forget about me, you will never forget that the woman you used, ripped her heart to shreds, and left for emotional and psychological death, is the same women that will be fucking your wife and tucking in your children into bed at night.

And that, my dear Jay, is what I call cosmic revenge. For, as long as I have the love of your wife and your kids, I will have all the time I need to make your life a living hell.

Hope you have a *sweet* life James, but know this, that Liz and I will be enjoying. . . *the sweeter side of deception.*"

She walked away, tossing the crumbled note at his feet that he had written that day he left her in Vancouver.

*An old chapter was finally closed and the new one could now begin.*

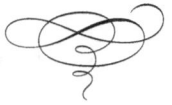

*Look out for the sequel!*
**Deception in the Details** — *Coming Soon!*

# Deception in the Details

## A Novella - Book Two

### by Avagaye Clarke-Heron

When Kayla Riviera finds out that her lover, the feisty, red-head (Elizabeth Westbrook) was the wife of James—the man who shattered her heart back in Vancouver, she swears to make his life a living hell. Elizabeth forgives Kayla for being the other woman in her marriage and they settle comfortably into their relationship with a burden-free heart, but little does Kayla know that this is only the beginning of a nightmare that she may never wake up from.

For news on upcoming books, sign up for
Avagaye Clarke-Heron's New Release updates
by emailing: inspirepublications1@gmail.com
or subscribe on her website:
www.inspirepublications.net

# Deception in the Details

A Novella - Book Two

by Avagaye Clarke-Heron

# Chapter I

On the drive to Liz's new home a strange silence settled in the car. Liz had asked Kayla why she stayed back to speak to James and Kayla told her she would tell her as soon as they got home.

"Liz I'm so excited that we are now free to be together."

"Hmm..." Liz said on a heavy exhale, looking straight ahead. The silence thickened and stretched.

Kayla knew what was eating Liz up inside but didn't know how to start.

"Take the right at the next intersection," Liz said in a gloomy tone. "It's the third house on the left. This is one of the properties my dad left behind," she added, as if she felt the awkwardness too. "You can pull up there in the driveway."

Kayla backed up the car in the driveway, Liz quickly got out and started unloading her things into the garage, Kayla could see from the look on her face that she was upset. She was desperate to clear the air. "Liz," she said grabbing onto Liz's hand as she tried to take the last box from the trunk of the car. "At least let me help you with this one because it a bit heavy." Liz looked at her, almost stating in her eyes that she didn't need her help, but Kayla held onto the box anyway helping her to lay it down in the garage. "I said I would tell you why I wanted to talk to James alone when we got home, and now we are home, you don't need to be mad at me because I *will* tell you." Liz threw her a skeptic look. "Trust me, I don't want to start the rest of our lives together with secrets because I know how dangerous that can be, please just let us go inside and I'll explain everything."

Liz pulled the garage door, hard, and strode to the front of the house to open the door. As she walked, her shoulders were visibly tense, which made her back arch slightly. Kayla followed behind her inside. "This is nice," Kayla said looking around at the picturesque, contemporary layout of Liz's sitting room. "Seems you have already made it ready to move in," she added, as she continued to observe the décor. The ash-grey laminate flooring anchored the white leather sofas flanked by a marble fireplace. A uniquely abstract-shaped coffee table stood in the middle of the room, and on top of the glass side tables were gorgeous lotus shaped lamps. Everything tied in beautifully with the luxurious, jasmine white drapes and almond white walls.

"Yeah," Liz replied with a dispassionate glance at the room. "I spent a few evenings here during the divorce process, fixing it up, making it ready for the kids. It wasn't much work to do, just a bit of dusting and re-shifting the furniture to my liking. It was one of those houses my dad would lease out, but I'm going to be using it for now because it's more of a family house than the others." After another drawn out pause, Liz cleared her throat. "So, should I get you something to drink?"

Kayla nodded to say yes, but Liz had already walked off to the kitchen. Kayla made her to way to the sitting area and sat on the edge of the couch. Liz came walking in with a bottle of red wine in one hand and two wine glasses in the other.

"Wine?" Kayla said looking at her, "well it definitely suits the occasion," she mumbled under her breath."

"What?" Liz was jumpy, a pained expression on her face.

"It's nothing," Kayla responded promptly; "I'd love some wine." Liz poured the wine and she sat on the couch next to Kayla.

Liz sloshed the wine a bit in the glass, took a sniff and sipped. "Well," she said, "since you are waiting for me to ask again... why you wanted to talk to James alone... you wanna tell me what is going on?"

Kayla took a sip from her own glass and looked at Liz. "For you to understand why I had to speak to James alone, you first need to know how it started."

"When you and I first met at *WhisPer*, you had asked me what was my story, I didn't know you then like I do now, so I didn't open up to you about my past. You told me then that the people you knew came to *WhisPer* to escape their realities and you were right. I was there because I was trying to somehow mend my broken heart. "You see," she shifted uncomfortably on the couch, "back in Vancouver, I met a guy, his name was Jay."

"What the heck does this have to do with you wanting to talk to James alone?" Liz interrupted, her eyes glared at Kayla.

"Just let me finish. It will all make sense if you'd just let me explain. Liz made a gesture as to say fine and Kayla continued to speak. "I met a guy in the coffee shop I stopped by every morning before I went to work, the lady at the coffee shop would normally have my coffee waiting for me at the same time every morning as she knew exactly what I needed. Decaf, one pump of hazel nut creamer and two blocks of sugar. One morning, I went in and it was packed, I signaled to Martha, the owner of the coffee shop, and she took up my coffee and placed it on the counter for me. Then out of nowhere this guy I had never seen in the shop before just walked up and held on to it. I assumed he was mistaking it for his, so I walked up to him and told him it was my coffee, he took a sip from it and said "no that's my coffee, 'decaf, one pump of hazel nut creamer and two blocks of sugar, just the way I like it.' I was a little taken aback that he had the same preference but I pointed to the cup where my name was clearly written on the side, close to the lid as Martha always did."

"He apologized, but was a little cynical, and I was pissed that he drank my coffee so I just turned around and walked out of the shop. I forgot all about it until a week later he showed up at my office offering to buy me another coffee and apologizing for his first impression at the coffee shop. Pretty soon I realized that the first impression I had of him was not right. He was sweet, considerate and he was not just another guy trying to get into my pants; at least that was what I thought then. Over time, as we kept seeing each other, we would talk about everything and he would listen and remember details. We dated on and off for the first two years and then things got more serious. We started sleeping with each other. I had things at his place and he left things at my condo. He told me he was an IT Consultant and that's why he travelled as often as he did, working with a number of companies in different countries. Frankly, it didn't bother me, and I didn't think much of it because it made our relationship exciting. When he was away, I would long for him, and when he came back the sex would be so amazing because we had time apart to miss each other."

I dated Jay for six years, and the longest he would stay out of Vancouver during that time was six months at a time. But then, he told me he had to go away for a family emergency for two years or more to take care of his family business and to support his brother who was going through a divorce. He suggested that we could see other people during that time apart, and that he would understand if I couldn't wait for him. Though I didn't know what our relationship would be like after that we still maintained our relationship over the phone. He would send me gifts on my birthday, and other special occasions and he convinced me to wait for him.

Six years of dating and two years of long-distance relationship, I was all in for this man for eight years, and when he came back to Vancouver I was convinced that he came back to marry me. I mean, if he didn't love me he could have blown me off when he went away, why come back? Why have me wait for him? After he had been back for some months, one weekend he told me he was taking me somewhere special. I felt within my heart that he was going to propose. He took me to a cabin by a beautiful lake, romanced me for the entire weekend, and on the morning, at the end of the weekend I got up with my hopes up ready for him to propose, only to find a note telling me that he went back to his wife and kids." Kayla broke down at this point and covered her face with her hands. Liz kept on staring at her in stony silence.

"I was devastated to say the least," she sniffled, letting her hands fall. "No one deserves to be used like that you know? I was hurt, I was angry, I was bitter, I was mad, even more so at myself for being so naïve and blinded by love. So, I took this promotion in California to start over; to try to get over the hurt, which for some time seemed impossible, because everywhere I went there was something that reminded me of him and how lonely and broken I was. "And then, I met you Liz, and I slowly started to be happy again, I started to heal, and I forgot about what Jay did to me until that night that you asked me to tail James for you."

# Chapter 2

"I don't understand. What happened when you tailed James?" Liz asked looking all confused,

"Liz there is no easy way to say this... but Jay... the guy who deceived me and took me for a ride, is your James... and I swear to you on my mother's grave, I did not know until that night I tailed James and to my surprise James was... Jay... James... oh, you know what I mean."

Liz sat her glass down on the table and looked at Kayla almost speechless.

"Say something!" Kayla said, holding onto Liz's hand.

"I hated her..." Liz responded with a look on her face as if she was staring into the past.

"Hated who?" Kayla asked confused.

"You, her, that woman who stole my husband's love away from me, I hated her, I hated you. Now you are telling me that you are that woman." Liz was near hysterical and turning beet red.

Kayla tried to calm her... "Liz, I was deceived by James too, please understand, when I met him I had no idea he was married, I told you the story of how we met for you to understand that I didn't even pursue this man. He found me, he made me love him, he took eight years of my life and threw it all into a blender along with my heart and liquefied it to nothing." She knelt in front of Liz. Please believe me when I tell you that if I had known that he was married I wouldn't have spent eight years loving this man... this should change nothing between us."

Liz got up from her seat, pacing around just trying to take it all in, then she just started to laugh. "Isn't it ironic? The Gods are indeed having a field day with my love life. What are the odds that the woman I hated for so long, that I thought about killing many times, the woman I lost my husband's love to is the woman that I fell in love with without even knowing it. God this is messed up on so many levels."

"I know this is messed up," Kayla said walking towards her, "and trust me when I found out I had so many mixed feelings about what this would mean for us. But Liz, how can you say he loved me, he didn't, he used me! Just like he used you, and Celia, and God knows how many others. He made me believe he was mine when all along he was married to you. He is sleeping with your family lawyer for God sakes, he didn't love me, so please don't say that."

Liz sat back down on the sofa and took another sip of her wine. "You don't understand," she said, "he loved you, the only reason he broke it off with her... with you... was because I made him, I gave him an ultimatum, break it off or lose everything... remember? He resented me after that and I believe that's why he went on this serial cheating to get back at me somehow for having him on a leash. I know my husband, and when he started the affair in Vancouver with you was the first time I knew I had lost him. You know the story Kayla, he changed... he didn't care for me anymore, he was risking his marriage, and his family to be with you. That's not just a silly affair, that's deeper than that. A silly affair is the one he was having with our lawyer, he didn't love her; it was just sex, to fill a need that I was not satisfying because I was still hurt that he didn't just have an affair with you, he fell in love."

Kayla sat beside Liz and took the glass from her, laying it back down on the coffee table. "None of that matters," she said to Liz. For all we know, you may have been reading too much into his 'supposed' love for me. I was on the other end, and I may have believed that then, but now I know it was just deception. Who forgets to tell someone, they claim to love, that they have a wife? When he dumped me in that note he left me at the cabin, he told me that when he met me he was going through a divorce, but if that was true why not say it then, why hide it? And judging from your story, when we met he was in Vancouver for the restructuring of your dad's companies not because he was going through a divorce like he said. Don't you get it? He never loved me. He was lying to me from the beginning, even before you gave him an ultimatum and that's not love in my book. So, again, I ask you, please stop saying that he loved me. The only reason I wanted to speak to him alone was to see the look on his face when he saw that we were together. I wanted to stick it to him, to point out the cosmic karma that was hitting him in the ass for what he did to me and that was it. If I had made you stay back while I said this to him you would have assumed the worst without knowing the entire story. I used to love Jay... James... whatever his name is, but now all I have in my heart for him is hate. I love you, and all I want is to be with you. Please don't let this change what we have found in each other, for each other. Please don't let the man that hurt us both be the one to come between us, or to change what we feel for each other."

Liz knew Kayla was right, and if she was completely honest with herself she would admit that it was satisfying to know how much more James would be hurting now that he knew she had not only left him with nothing but left him for the woman he broke their marriage for. The thought secretly made her smile inside, among other things that were brewing in her mind. She looked Kayla squarely in the face. "You are right. He used us both. It would be unfair to blame you for any of this because you were the victim; whether he had truly loved you is insignificant because it was based on deception. Let's just forget about James for now, we know we haven't heard the last of him, so let's just not work ourselves up about him until we have to deal with him."

Kayla hugged and kissed her in a gesture of relief. She was happy that Liz was willing to understand, and to forget about it and just move on with their lives without reliving James's deception drama.

Even though Kayla was relieved, she couldn't help but think that Liz handled the situation better than she had imagined. She had seemed so level-headed about it even while voicing her concerns. She quickly shrugged the thought from her mind as she told herself she was over-thinking it. She spent the rest of the evening helping Liz to unpack and just enjoying each other's company, basking in the feeling of finally being free to be together.

# Chapter 3

James did not sleep well that night, he sat on the sofa in the living room just gazing at the television but not hearing a word, drinking glass after glass of bourbon. He couldn't make sense of it all, Kayla and Elizabeth. How was Kayla and Elizabeth together, how did they even meet? How was it that Kayla was the one who got evidence of him cheating with Celia? Was Liz and Kayla working together to make his life miserable, does Liz know that Kayla was the one he cheated with back in Vancouver? There were so many questions on his mind but no answers and it made him miserable. He gazed over at his phone, and noted the constant message notifications and missed calls but he didn't care. He laid down on the couch hugging the bourbon bottle. "Damn you Elizabeth!" He screamed, jumping up and tossing the bottle across the room. "Damn you!"

He made his way up the stairs, staggering, sweaty and confused. He needed to speak to Kayla, but how to do it was the question. Where would he start? He plopped himself down in bed, his head pounding, and stomach churning from the drinking. His eyes slowly dimmed, and he passed out.

A loud pounding on the door woke him up, and the sudden jolt of his head as he tried to rise, left a hammering ache on the left side of his head. He grabbed his phone to look at the time, it was 5:30 am. He held his hand to his head where the pain was as he walked over to the closet to get a shirt. He managed to throw on the shirt and made his way downstairs. The knocking at the door only got louder. "I'm coming!" he shouted, as he made his way towards the door. When he opened the door it was Celia. Her emotions were not easily hidden on her innocent-looking face. Pain was evident in her honey-brown eyes and in the downward curve of her full lips.

"What are you doing here?" he asked, grabbing her by the hand and pulling her in. He looked over her head to make sure no one saw her enter his house. Before she could respond, he said, "This is against the rules" as he closed the door. "You know my house is off limits."

"That was when you were legally married." Celia pulled her hand from his grasp. "Besides, I have been calling, and leaving messages for you to call me back, for over two days now, and you haven't picked up any of my calls or called me back."

"Really?" James looked at her annoyed. "You expect me to have a clear head to take calls, and have small talks with my mistress after everything that has happened over the last couple of months. Are you crazy?"

"I'm not the one that is crazy James, your wife is. I received an email from her, she's threating to have me subpoenaed by the Supreme Court. It's not bad enough that she is suing me for violation of trust and alienation, and a hoard of other things; she's going after my credentials. She's trying to have me disbarred for desecration of the ethics of my profession."

James sat down, looking up at her in disbelief. "Can she do that?" What a pickle they have gotten themselves in; he was almost feeling sorry for her.

"Technically, yes, she can, because you both were my clients, and were legally married. I was trusted to advise you both, based on the ethical code(s) I operated under as a divorce attorney, plus it is especially frowned upon for divorce attorneys to have sexual relations with their clients. James, I can handle losing my job with my firm here in California, but I cannot handle being disbarred. Do you know what that would mean for me? I won't be able to practice law anywhere else; I'd be finished!"

"I know what it means Celia, just let me think." James got up and began pacing the bare wooden floor that was now devoid of the expensive rugs that he and Elizabeth had acquired over the years.

"You have to do something James," she implored. You still share custody of the kids with her, right? So, that means you both still have a relationship. Please talk to her, convince her to withdraw. I know she hates me and she has all right to, but destroying my life is going too far. Plus, you need to take some responsibility for this too James. If you hadn't shown up at my house that night we wouldn't be in this mess. We had those rules for a reason James, we never meet at our homes, we never book hotel rooms with credit cards, and we never meet close to home, this is all your fault!" Celia shouted at him, bursting into tears, her hands trying tirelessly to swipe her dangling auburn curls from her wet face. James tried to console her by reaching out to hold her but she wouldn't let him touch her.

"My life is ruined too you know," he said in an upset tone, I have no job, I have practically nothing, the life I was used to is now swept from under my feet, I am just as lost as you are."

"You haven't lost everything James," Celia replied angrily. At least you are still a lawyer, she didn't push to have you disbarred, you can join another firm in a heartbeat, but what about me? If she goes through with this I will never be able to work anywhere."

"How long ago did she send you that email?" James asked.

"About three days ago. Why?"

"Just thinking," James answered, "That means she sent you the email before she moved her things from the house yesterday. She has thought this through, and I seriously doubt if I'll have any luck convincing her otherwise. We haven't even decided on the custody schedule as yet so I don't know when I'll even see her. I'm waiting on my lawyer to contact me about the final decision. Celia, I'm really sorry about this, I am, but I can't risk getting further on Elizabeth's bad side. I can't risk losing joint custody of my kids. How do you think she'll take it if I try to talk to her about the welfare of my 'mistress'? I can't promise you anything at least not now, give me some time to get myself together, to work things out regarding my kids and I'll see what can be done, but no promises."

"How did I get here?" Celia muttered under her breath, "from a highly respectable, sought after attorney to the woman who is about to lose it all, and for what? What did I even see in you to risk my career, my reputation?"

"Let's not go down that road," James interjected. "We are both in a sticky situation because of a decision we both consciously made knowing the consequences; so please let's not start pointing fingers, Ok? I said I would try to talk to her but I'm not making any promises, let me just try to get myself together and see what happens over the next couple of weeks. Besides, she has only emailed you, doesn't seem as if she has made any motion against you yet with the courts so let's not jump the gun. Just go home, get some rest, so that you can think straight to try and find a legal way out of this. There must be a way, just go think about it. Talk to some of the attorneys in your circle, and I'll try and reach out to some friends. I'll let you know if I come up with anything and you should do the same."

James kissed Celia on the forehead and walked her to the door. When she left, he couldn't help but blame himself for all that was happening.

What was he to do?

He was at the mercy of Elizabeth, just as Celia was, and on top of that Kayla threatened to make his life a living hell. He felt sorry for Celia, but he had no idea where to start to help her. If Elizabeth had threatened to destroy her, there was nothing he could do, or say now, that would change her mind. He walked over to the broom closet and grabbed the dust bin and went across the room where he had tossed the bourbon bottle, he picked up the larger pieces of broken glass and scooped up the splinters.

As he emptied the dust bin in the kitchen garbage can his phone rang. It was his divorce attorney with the call he had been expecting. "Hey James, its Noel, I have some great news for you, your wife's divorce attorney and I have come to a final decision based on your wife's wishes and the welfare of your kids. If you meet me at my office at noon today, I can fill you in and hand over the documentation you will need regarding the joint custody."

"That sounds great, Noel," James replied. "I will see you at noon, take care now."

For news on upcoming books, sign up for
Avagaye Clarke-Heron's New Release updates
by emailing: inspirepublications1@gmail.com
or subscribe on her website:
www.inspirepublications.net

# Avagaye Clarke-Heron

Avagaye Clarke-Heron is a business professional by day and a writer by night as well as a wife and mom all year round.

Jamaican born, she moved to the Cayman Islands, in 2014 with her husband, to pursue her career ambitions.

Avagaye holds a Master's degree in General Management and a Bachelor's degree in Finance.

Before she started writing romantic suspense, she experimented with various occupations: Property Management, Accounting, Retail Business Analyst... and she has even published a children's book, but her favorite job is the one she's now doing full time—writing romance.